The God Pot

The God Pot

Stephen Lloyd Webber

TMMW

Stephen Lloyd Webber/TMMW LLC

www.tmmw.io

Publisher's Note: This is a work of fiction. Names, characters, places, and incidents are a product of the author's imagination. Locales and public names are sometimes used for atmospheric purposes. Any resemblance to actual people, living or dead, or to businesses, companies, events, institutions, or locales is completely coincidental.

The God Pot / Stephen Lloyd Webber – First Edition

ISBN 979-8-9941408-1-9

The weather was colder than he'd expected. Moony struggled to remove his gloved hands from his fleece-lined pockets. Freedom would be more comfortable, though he had no plans for it.

His girlfriend, Celia, was swinging herself along on his arm, chatting on the phone. He recognized a phrase that usually necessitated a human emotional response. She had said, "I love you."

He had turned to her before realizing she hadn't been speaking to him. She had another lover, he remembered. A woman named Deb. He remembered he didn't mind.

The couple walked across the snowy parking lot of Sod Hill, the golf-themed apartment complex where he lived. The lot used artificial grass instead of asphalt, and the turf remained adequately verdant despite a few years of tire wear. The golf theme was purely cosmetic—Moony doubted half the tenants had ever held a club. The apartments were bottom-tier rentals, the kind of units that attracted people who needed cheap more than they needed nice. A few renters took advantage of the blank facades of their units to hang sports banners, which raised their spirits during the playing season.

Moony's gaze traveled from the artificial turf upward to Celia's boots, her jeans, her hips, eyes out of habit roving the rest of her body. He thought about women in general. The odor of smoke from a chimney wafted his way, and the smell triggered a memory.

Four months earlier, before moving out of his parents' estate— a sprawling property within spitting distance of the Federal Center, with security that would make most embassies envious— he spent the night celebrating his college graduation by trying to drink at every bar in suburbia.

Sod Hill's nearest bar, Frog House, was the last on the list. He remembered having sex with a woman he met dancing who called herself Hello Kitty. Everyone else called her Kitty. She was middle aged and smelled like cedar. Celia, even after swimming or sex or a shower, always managed to smell like new Gap clothing.

When Kitty was naked and he had fooled around with her under the fluorescent lights of the bar's back office, it was a struggle for him to stay oriented amid her foresty scent. There had either been no lock on the door or he hadn't bothered to find the latch. When Kitty's undaunted older sister barged in, she extended her hand, expecting a handshake. Moony, kneeling on the desk between Kitty's baby-oiled ankles, craned his neck around to see her. He extended his left hand since it was not otherwise occupied, and the woman shook it vigorously as if something were now a done deal.

Kitty's sister, the intruder, introduced herself as the Gypsy, owner of some sort of rare artsy theater in Tulsa, Oklahoma. Her accent—Eastern European, possibly Romanian—stuck out to Moony's ear. His father had insisted on language training since childhood: Russian, Mandarin, and Spanish. Just more family business prep.

The Gypsy scanned Kitty and assessed Moony. He looked average in some ways and above average in others, with the kind of face that could blend in or stand out, depending on what was needed. She thought about whether he could be trusted, and whether she could rely on him as a business partner.

"Are you enjoying yourselves?" she asked. Moony nodded. He was glad to see Kitty nod.

The Gypsy called Kitty toward her. The dark sisters moved to a place where Moony could still see but not hear them. He caught fragments—or thought he did: something about Polish contracts, Estonian servers, Brussels deadlines—or maybe just *Polish*, *Estonia*, and *Brussels*, filled in by his own expectations of what conversations like this should contain.

His father's voice echoed in his head: "People will always want access to our networks."

He admired Kitty's nudity; she moved easily in the fluorescent light, comfortable in a space that should have made anyone self-conscious. Then the Gypsy moved away from her whispered conference with Kitty and positioned herself in the corner of the room, arms crossed, watching.

Moony waited for Kitty to say something—to acknowledge that the situation had become strange, or to suggest they continue this another time. Instead, she pulled him back toward her with a smile that suggested this was all perfectly normal.

He glanced at the Gypsy. She hadn't moved.

"Don't mind her," Kitty whispered. "She's just curious about you."

Moony had been raised to believe that unusual situations were tests—that the correct response was to proceed as if nothing were unusual at all. So he did. He told himself this was sophistication, European permissiveness, something beyond his suburban experience that he should rise to meet, even though the woman insisted on being called a name he'd been taught was a slur.

The Gypsy stood in the corner watching them have sex, motionless except for her eyes, like a director watching actors hit their marks. It had definitely been weird for Moony, but not weird enough to get him to do anything to change it.

Later, as he was leaving, the Gypsy pressed a card into his palm. It contained only a phone number and a small logo: a theatrical mask with a third eye in the center. No name, no company.

"Perhaps we'll meet again when you're ready to discuss real opportunities."

A thrill shot through him, but Moony kept his face blank. This was standard procedure, wasn't it? He pocketed the card without looking at it, the way he imagined seasoned operatives did. At the time, Moony had been confident that his father was about to send him on a job to help with the family interests in Ecuador. He was sure that any day he would become immensely important and useful.

Four months passed, with his family telling him nothing beyond the vague reassurances and empty updates that kept him at arm's length. Each call was the same dance—hints about "developments" and "timing" that never materialized into actual directives.

The silence felt deliberate. Maybe this was just another test, seeing how long he'd wait in the suburbs before cracking.

❖ ❖ ❖

The lover Celia was chatting intimately with was Deb Infield, co-manager of Sod Hill, a woman she had met and subsequently made eyes at while lounging alone near the apartment complex's golf club–shaped pool.

These things do happen.

The two women, one (Deb) much older than the other, had the sorts of things in common that set them into high echelons of archetypal attractiveness. They found each other endlessly mesmerizing and psychologically beautiful, which tinged the object of their affection with the styling of an opposite. To gaze at each other provided a challenging glimpse into a depth of resistance within themselves. Each woman saw the effects of time and generation, how their tastes and affectations had influenced the secret and sumptuous core of femininity that each embodied for the other. The pairing afforded both women an opportunity to striptease the boundaries of common relationships: mother, daughter, lover, competitor, confidant, seductress, protégé.

Moments after Celia had spoken to Deb her heartfelt "I love you," Moony achieved silent elation by extricating himself from his own pockets. He linked his arm with hers, partly because he felt romantic, partly because he wanted to soothe her incessant swinging. The joining of arms infected him, her happy motion spurred him into silliness, and they began trotting to the bar like underworked horses put out to graze.

Quite simply, Celia was stoned. She hung up her phone and imagined that the two of them were innocent civilians in post–World War II Germany. In her mind, the backdrop of suburban Denver took on a menacing hue. The sky grew dark with a distant red imminence. Unlike most people, when Celia's mind wandered into fantasy, she chose to stay there. Squinting her eyes, she saw a myriad of swastikas and mustard gas. Fumes rose from the artificial turf to her nose in ferocious wisps. For comfort, she squeezed the bicep nearest to her hands, looking at Moony as her one-man army, soldier, and lonesome hero. His bomber jacket was not just for looks—she glanced down at his acid-washed and artificially worn designer blue jeans—he would need to get some new pants.

"Oh, Bomber, I don't know if we'll make it into France alive," she said to Moony, squeezing his shoulder in goofy desperation.

He looked at her without a clue, wondering if this was a hint that she needed something.

She deftly maneuvered herself into a hug.

When moved by emotion he couldn't name, Moony had the habit of pulling his face into unconventional expressions without being aware of it. Just now, he rolled his lips toward his teeth and kept them pressed together as he brought his jaw down. A person standing at a distance might have seen in him a well-groomed Tom Waits.

They trotted into Frog House as Perry, the bar's owner and co-manager of Sod Hill, dimmed the lights to a romantic level in preparation for the screening—ineffectively, due to the abundance of lumens flooding in through the bar's floor-to-ceiling untinted windows. A morass of plasma and ancient big-screen rear projection televisions all showed the DVD menu of the classic *King Kong*. The proposal to screen movies in the bar on numerous televisions all at once owed its existence to Perry. The inevitable failure of the proposal also came from Perry. The plan was to screen an old movie, hold a discussion break, and then show a remade version of the same film. This, he believed, would bring in a more diverse and artistic crowd to the bar, which lately had not been doing well at all.

Twice a week were the Guaranteed No-Patron Days—the bartender went to work when the bar opened and turned on the lights to make it appear as if he was present, but actually, he had gone back home. He would return when it was time for the next shift to begin, when usually the next bartender would do the same.

Perry's employees had shown him strong disagreement regarding the notion that screening movies this early in the day would be a good idea, but he defended himself from this abuse by altering his self-image as pioneer of an idea. Any idea, once owned by a pioneer, could become something enduring and worthwhile. Earlier that week, Perry had been explaining his vision to Josh, who was cleaning the pool, and to Moony, who was wondering why he'd stopped by. Perry's first-thought-best-thought name had been the Electric Megaplex, but Moony shook his head.

"Amphitheater," Moony said.

At once, the idea had become Perry's. "You see," Perry explained, turning to Josh with gathering enthusiasm, "because frogs are amphibians, this being the Frog House."

"Why not the Ribbitorium?" Josh suggested.

Perry considered this. "Not artsy enough, Josh, but I like the hustle."

Moony attended the screenings because he had nothing better to do, which was exactly how he'd arranged his life. He was here out of a vague sense of neighborly obligation and because Perry had mentioned it three times that week, which in Moony's experience meant someone really wanted something. He also believed, despite appearances, that there was more to Perry than met the eye.

Deb, Perry's ex-wife and Sod Hill's other co-manager, wrangled with the cords behind the DVD player to get the audio to work with the bar's sound system, peacock-feather earrings tickling the delicate blue veins of her cleavage. Today was the third of January, which meant that she should have been preparing the list of tenants who had not yet paid their rent so that they could be telephoned and appropriately reprimanded, but having heard Perry go on about how he had pioneered his idea got her to think twice about spending another few hours on something she'd only repeat in a month. She decided instead that she would stop being the bad guy.

The truth was she'd never wanted to be anybody's bad guy—not her first husband's, not her tenants'. She'd wanted to be a kindergarten teacher once, but through an odd series of events—a semester abroad in Nepal, a surprise reunion with her estranged father followed by a whirlwind romance with an extended relative of Mick Jagger—she'd met Perry while doing administrative work for a local college and decided that her best life would be one that allowed her to serve as a source of love, pleasure, and beauty for those around her.

Work was work, and life meant the pursuit of connection. Though drawn to dramatic entanglements everywhere else, in the bedroom, Deb was the most generous and secure lover in the world.

It was a plus for her to see that Celia had arrived.

❖ ❖ ❖

Waiting for the movie to begin, Moony was restless, even though he had just done all the things that made him happy. He'd had sex and played *Double Dragon* on Super Nintendo, a game he believed centered his chi, provided he performed well at it.

Still adjusting to his life's downward trajectory after moving into his Sod Hill apartment, his personal gravity and energy flow were so out of whack that, in his words, they *sucked*. But his present situation was not effective at disturbing him in a long-lasting way. He was a person who ate when he got hungry (lately, a lot) and slept when he got tired (ten hours a night on a luxuriously padded mattress); he left all the other things to take care of themselves. Moony will live healthily to the ripe old age of ninety-one.

Celia, who was present for the sex but not the video game playing, was not in the mood for complaining, either—she had just narrowly escaped a troubling situation involving a would-be suiter, Heath Johannson, the Swedish-American who made meth in the apartment across the hall from Moony's.

Heath arrived for the screening early, not because he was punctual but because he was strung out and had trouble telling accurate time. You see, he was uncertain whether the minutes went forward or backward as they approached 10:30. He had some skill with a pencil and could draw a diagram to explain this phenomenon, but the resulting illustration would never be sufficient grounds to prove his theories on space-time. Heath's brain had trained itself to misfire synapses and crosslink neurons.

At 10:03, Heath wrote this note and taped it on Moony's door, apartment Q303:

King Gong ! Knock Knock ! one one Read this

He rang the doorbell and retreated into his own apartment, which bubbled like a laboratory. He licked his lips, caked in a powdery substance that resembled baking soda except for its electric graveyard taste.

He looked out the peephole.

Moony's wooden door remained closed. Heath felt footsteps tromping up the stairs. A hand rapped lightly on his door.

He flung it open. Shadrack, a five-foot-four amphetamine connoisseur who had developed the useful habit of being in several places at once without anyone quite remembering how he'd gotten there or what exactly he'd said, entered Heath's apartment.

"I saw Lee today," Shadrack beamed proudly as he entered, "and that lady can sure talk cars. I asked her whether I should hook up the *conversion kit* to my dually." He winced and snorted as he screamed the words *conversion kit*. There was no reason for him to do this. You know it. I know it.

Moony, sporting six-pack abs and army-green boxer briefs, opened his door and nodded dully to Heath, who watched manically from across the hall. Moony's physique was hard to beat, considering the amount of discipline he put toward perfecting it, which was none—at least not anymore. Years of expensive private school athletics and summer camps had built the foundation: martial arts classes his father had insisted would build "the mind of a Caesar," extreme fitness programs, wilderness survival programs, even some tactical paintball courses that Moony was certain were run by retired Delta Force operators.

But since moving to Sod Hill, he had been deliberately letting himself go, making earnest investments toward a beer gut and the soft edges that might help him blend in to civilian life. The six-pack was proving stubbornly resistant to neglect.

He shook his head at Heath's face (emphatic, yet stone still) and returned to his apartment. Heath hopped to life and rang Moony's doorbell, standing unacceptably close to the door.

Moony answered.

Heath motioned toward the note. "Somebody left this for you," he said and nibbled his dirty knuckles. His teeth looked very straight because they had all fallen out. He wore dentures.

Shadrack continued as if Heath were listening. "She said I just might be dumber than Heath when he put a *potato* in his own Corvette's tailpipe. Remember that?"

Moony read the note aloud in a smoky monotone voice: "'King Gong, Knock knock, one one, read this.' Hmm."

His average eyes inquired at Heath, inches from his face; Heath's body odor smelled like battery acid and legumes.

Shadrack wasn't to be ignored. "'Member the potato?"

Glancing over at Shadrack tugging on Heath's arm, at Shadrack's half-opened button-down Dickies work shirt, Moony's eyes landed on the man's chest, home to blurred and faded tattoos depicting what Moony would describe as "gross-looking gremlin skulls." On the forehead of one of these, in Cyrillic characters, was the word *Rook* and an Orthodox cross. The kind of garbage that meant nothing to most people but disconcerted Moony, because he was familiar with the word as a nickname for the AK-47.

Shadrack laughed, sneezed, laughed some more, his eyes never quite meeting Moony's but somehow taking an interest in everything about the doorframe, the apartment number, the sight lines down the hallway. Even for someone tweaking on amphetamines, his peripheral awareness was remarkably acute.

Moony read the note again. The text meant nothing to him. He understood that Heath's brain was a junkyard of chemicals.

Heath broke the silence, gesturing toward the note as if it were a bird about to fly away. "At the Frog House, if you want to watch *King Kong*." He blew a hard kiss to the note, and yes, it flew from Moony's hand.

Shadrack tugged on Heath's arm. He laughed. He sneezed. He laughed some more.

Moony felt the urge to kick the man. He considered the note's proposition for a moment. He looked at his wrist, where there was no Tag Heuer watch anymore. *Perhaps Celia borrowed it*, he thought, as part of what he believed to be the female desire to adorn oneself in the clothing and apparatus of the boyfriend.

Celia was in Moony's apartment. Heath saw her there, lazily attempting some sort of yoga. She was not naked but had the tousled look about her that implied that had been recently nude because of sexual circumstances. Celia had been regularly sleeping with Moony since two days after he'd moved in, which was about three months ago. Heath had tried unsuccessfully to get Celia to sleep with him two months ago. Only Heath, Celia, and God himself were aware of the overlap.

When Heath matched eyes with Celia in Moony's apartment and deduced that she had been naked and/or tousled, he felt something akin to jealousy broil in his belly. Celia recognized this as a troubling situation, doubly so, as she recalled that, on the day Moony moved into Sod Hill, he'd accidentally backed his car into Heath's Corvette. Although he'd paid for the repairs, Heath seemed unable to connect the two events: the accident Moony had caused, which angered him, and the gift of money Moony had bestowed, which overwhelmed him with gratitude.

Moony had told himself his move to Sod Hill was strategic—low profile, establishing distance from his family. But if he thought about it directly, he'd have to admit that something in him had broken, and he didn't know how to fix it. So instead he thought, *Deep cover. Sleeper protocol. Awaiting activation.*

The mythology was a room he could live in. He'd met Celia in the hallway that same day. They struck up a conversation, one thing led to another, and she moved in with him. Beginnings can happen just like that.

While Celia yogically pondered the beginnings of her relationship with Moony and whether God had dealt Heath a fair life, something biblical happened. Flames erupted from inside Heath's apartment, possibly caused by a heavily modified electric blanket in the bathtub, which was near an overfilled and uncorked bottle of ether.

The look of horror in Moony's eyes was mistakeable, considering it was a look he had constructed in imitation of Bruce Willis's role as Detective Lieutenant John McClane in *Die Hard*. But the whoosh, coupled with the pupils of Moony's eyes shrinking to pinpricks at the brightness of the flame, were enough to make Heath's brain forget that he had been talking to Shadrack, had written Moony a note, and had seen Celia.

He rushed to one of the six commercial-grade fire extinguishers in his living room and finished off the blaze like a professional. Moony had headed toward Heath's apartment to feign assistance but stopped when Celia called for him to come back and close the door.

The brief discussion he had with Celia revealed that Heath was, in fact, a professional fireman who began taking amphetamines as a means to stay awake and ready for danger and that he had an unrequited crush on Celia—she told Moony she believed it was best for them not to be too showy about their relationship in front of him since it would make him jealous, and she was concerned he might be a dangerous person. Seeing Moony's complete lack of fear led her to initiate another round of brief lovemaking.

At 10:56, Moony and Celia were dressed and of a mind to see the original *King Kong* movie.

❖ ❖ ❖

Moony sat in Frog House waiting for the movie to begin, his skin pricked by the metallic reverberations of the room's dull conversations and the awkward heating ducts.

"*Oh, home on the ranch,*" he sang to himself, reminded that his younger brother Alex was on his way to a death metal concert in Chicago because he needed to (in his own words) elope into rebellious despair.

Moony thought of his older sister Yvette. She, he supposed, had moved beyond the need to rebel, in that she had made what the family called her "final gesture." She had killed herself.

When it turned out the attempt was successful, Moony had been the first to know because when he'd entered his number into her phone, he'd labeled himself "Daddy-Pops" as a joke. So when the Montana police called, it was Daddy-Pops who got the news, and Daddy-Pops who had to break it to the family.

People always wanted to know if she'd been of sound mind, if there had been cries for help. The truth was more complicated. Yvette had been trying to extract herself from the family's Montana operation. She'd talked to Moony about it, and he'd never understood.

"If you leave, it means we never see you again," he'd said.

"You know I'll always love you."

Those words had cut him. He refused to accept them.

"Life's no better out there. Out there, you're nobody."

By "out there," he meant the world of ordinary people who did not have powerful connections and bottomless wealth.

"I've seen how the sausage gets made," she'd said. "I can't stomach it anymore."

"If you don't grind the meat, someone else will."

Moony meant that if exploitation was profitable, someone would always volunteer to do the exploiting.

Yvette went on, "I want to be my own person. Even if that makes me a nobody to you."

"You've been prepared for big things since birth. You think you can just pretend none of this matters? People like us don't get to abandon our role in shaping history," he'd told her. "We can't put the genie back in the bottle," Moony had loved his sister and recognized in her someone purer than himself. He wished she had been less pure. He'd hoped to make her that way by reminding her what it meant to be family.

Yvette, in seclusion on the other end of the phone, drove to the same hill a few miles north of town where she had attempted suicide three weeks before by swallowing pills, which her body decided it wasn't ready for and hence regurgitated. She'd spoken to her brother in a clear voice: "Which do you think is better, being alive or dead?" The breeze at her elevation blew yellow pollen-filled debris onto her windshield.

"Dead, probably," he'd said. He'd laughed.

"I'm not scared of death, I don't think." Her car's tires crunched over the gravel as she turned onto a familiar road.

"That's cool, sis. Probably, I should let you go."

"Talk to you later." Within an hour, the blue sky saw her spirit leave its body.

When their mother, Joanne, found out, she locked herself in the guest house and cried for the better part of two days. She decided there would be a cremation and absolutely no funeral service. She never questioned Alex or Moony or wondered why Moony was the first to know. She wouldn't entertain any possibility that Yvette's feelings may have been justified, even though little could be said to defend Yvette's actions.

Joanne wouldn't entertain these thoughts. She insisted on being happy. She was too angry to allow her happiness to be sacrificed as the effect of any circumstance.

❖ ❖ ❖

Deb cheered for herself after hearing the bark of audio, which could only mean she'd wired the equipment correctly. She spotted Moony and Celia, who sat post-coitally in a sort of love nest—a rough circle of empty chairs. At the sudden flash of the *King Kong* title screen, she became self-conscious of her excessive cheer. She thought of herself as appropriately inhibited.

"You got the note!" She ran toward Moony, arms outstretched.

Still seated, he gave her a one-handed hug, wondering why she had said that since he hadn't gotten a note from her, but then he remembered other times Heath had removed a message from Moony's door only to replace it with one of his own. Out of principle, Moony tried to enjoy the feeling of Deb's epic tits against the side of his face as he hugged her, but it didn't work. He hoped his assigned distance from the family business wasn't dulling his ability to enjoy the satisfactions life brought his way.

He'd chosen to live here at Sod Hill as a temporary fuck you to the man, all the while thinking of himself as a sleeper asset. A low-rent apartment complex in suburban Denver was in no one's book a worthy position for someone raised in the tradecraft of Adams Minerals. But he'd moved here after his sister's death thinking it would give him a chance to detox from the adversarial and elitist worldview of his upbringing, and it had.

The detox had been so effective he'd unraveled much of his motivation to advance his life in any given direction. Before graduation, his father had assured him that in short order, he'd be on his way to his first major assignment. His only source of pride had been to wait for information about the Ecuadorian affair. But he'd seen signs that his father's assurance of an upcoming assignment was actually a tease.

It bothered him that he'd chosen the cover of directionless trust fund kid and had, in a disturbingly short time, become one with the part. Moony suspected he had been cosmically right in his choice to live among these board gamers, addictive chemical solopreneurs, and tech support workers because he wasn't cut out for the high stakes of the family business or that his father hadn't activated him because Moony was too much of a believer to be an operator. There was so much about his family's operation he didn't understand, and he suspected that was by design—keep the heir in the dark until he proved himself worthy of the truth.

Deb let Moony go, and he appraised her. She was twice his age, and it showed somewhat in her face, but her body was that of a twenty-year-old.

Celia smiled at their hug since what she saw looked endearing. But Perry, standing in the center of the room smacking evenly on cinnamon chewing gum, knew enough about Deb to feel jealous. The two of them had gotten into the business deal as husband and wife seven years ago. Three years ago, Deb had decided to divorce Perry and try again with her first husband, the man Deb had been cheating on (with Perry) since day one of their marriage, though she and Perry still saw each other on occasion since they were so proximal.

Perry stretched his hands out and welcomed everyone, then paused for a moment, realizing that he recognized every face he saw. Anyone who cared could detect his disappointment at giving a free movie screening to the same audience the bar had been supporting already. His heart was sick with years of unarticulated sadness.

He gave a big smile anyway and said "Enjoy!" Moony believed this was good advice.

Perry drew the blinds to darken the room. Frog House's plasma screens bounced light off the faces of the dozen tenants who had come here on Sunday morning to watch a movie for free. Light refracted off the bar's emerald walls and floor and soaked into the black ceiling.

The bar had gone industrial-cold, like a loading dock in winter. The heater rattled awake and pushed warmth that smelled of burned cardboard, basement corners, and the inside of an empty egg carton.

Moony paid close attention to the screen to learn what he could from *King Kong*. He compared himself to the ape and approved the results. He felt both like a giant and an outcast.

Though Moony's parents had taken him off their visible payrolls, he still earned a living by visiting the ATM to withdraw a reasonable portion of the inheritance money that came from his great-grandfather Thurman Bloodgood Adams, who had the luck and keen eye to profit from Depression-era troubles. Moony shared all the good genes with his great-grandfather and saw himself as having evolved to the point of realizing that if he did not need to work for money, he would not. He had believed that as someone destined for real power, he could afford to be big, wild, and dumb and would see what the universe offered him in exchange.

As bullets from biplanes filled the giant ape, the power in Frog House cut off. Perry jumped to action and ran through the bar's darkness to open the blinds. No light filtered in.

Celia snickered—she was nervous.

Perry, the expert, opened the front door to investigate. A massive snowdrift had formed a wall against the bar.

There had been signs of a pending snowstorm, sure. But none of the people in the bar could be counted among those who kept track of weather or who even believed that something like weather might affect them personally.

"Christ." If Perry had been in the Wild West, he would have spat on the ground. But since he wasn't, he snapped his fingers, and they sounded as if he was trying to strike a match. The wall of snow begged for his body warmth.

The bar projected a startling and vacuous energy without the familiar sound of gas heaters, refrigerator motors, and an occasional pop from an ice machine or radiator. Everyone sat on their asses—not many situations made Moony want his occasional cigarette more than the sight of boring stability. His hands needed something to do, so he sat on them. He didn't want to have an addiction.

Celia made a joke. It wasn't funny, but Deb and Moony laughed with her a bit. Moony was the first to stop laughing. For the first time in his life, he caught a glimpse of real darkness—here, of all places, sitting in a dive bar on a Sunday morning.

Perry appraised the smooth, subtly cleft wall of packed snow. It was a wonder it had snowed at all, and certainly that it had snowed this much—enough to seal a doorway entirely—and that it had come to such a drift. It had an aesthetically sublime curve to it, a perfect gradient from the ground to the door frame. Perry had to admire it even as he realized they were trapped. To him, it looked like the ass of a huge, reclining snow goddess. The snowdrift groaned and dumped a mound into the bar's open doorway.

"Christ," he said again and struggled to get the door closed. At first, it looked like he had it under control; he was just slipping on the snow, which anyone is apt to do, but then he tumbled face forward into it.

Much, much more snow rolled over him in a thick, suffocating dome. His natural impulse to close the door overrode his perception that he was pushing, rather than pulling, and when it closed, he had sealed himself outside the building. Slippery, shivering, and frustrated, he could no longer find the entrance.

From the inside, Moony ambled to the rescue, taking a little extra time to glance back at everyone else who sat without doing anything. *They're in movie-watching mode,* he thought. *Well, so am I. Life is unfair.*

He freed Perry by swinging the door open and offering his hand.

Standing on scared-to-death feet, Perry was the Yeti shivering in coveralls. His face, especially his beard, was caked in snow.

"Jesus Christ," said Perry. Luckily for his credibility, his tears were disguised behind clumps of white snow. He stood like an accused child.

Moony asked if it would be all right if he had a cigarette, but the landlord shook his head.

"Well, I'll be!" said Deb. What Deb meant was that she'd be *damned*, but Deb was horrified at bad language, especially the word *damn*. Fear of damnation was what propelled her through adolescence and kept her from having a steady relationship with boys. Relishing the allure of damnation was what propelled her to have relations with her best friends' boyfriends and, therefore, kept her from steady friendships with girls.

She raced toward the bar and mixed herself a drink. All this excitement encouraged her to crave the state she normally associated with excitement, which was the state of being intoxicated.

"Anybody care for a drink? I'm having one."

Appraising the people in the bar, Moony felt like one of those reptilian elites from conspiracy theories—cold blooded and watching from above. To him all normal people were weird, but Sod Hill was a petri dish richly cultured with unusuals. He sized them up, each in turn:

"I'll have a vodka tonic," answered Josh, a satanist.

"I'll have a Tom Collins," said Jon-Jon, a part-time clown.

"Whiskey and diet Coke," said Yvonne, a quiet girl.

"Do you have Bud Light in a can?" asked a person without friends.

"Guinness," said another.

"Hamm's," said another, louder than the former.

"Sam Adams, please," said a man who resembled the God painted on the ceiling of the Sistine Chapel.

Heath went to sleep in the corner. He had been awake for three days, and enough was enough. He laid his head on a book entitled *Top Dog*, a book whose interior was more or less the same as this one, if you can believe it.

Through his snow beard, Perry muttered to Deb as to the existence of a few dozen tea light candles under the bar. The candles brought a ghastly sort of illumination to the very green-tiled, very wood-paneled, very dusty bar.

Moony was familiar with mixing drinks and entertaining guests, and so he proved helpful to Deb, who believed him to be a real Swiss army knife of gentlemanliness. He didn't mind entertaining her belief that he was something other than himself. The theme of what he was taught during childhood was *Good things come to those who take and take and take*. It was a warped kind of Americanism.

For Moony's eleventh birthday, when his parents hired Digital Underground to play, he asked the band if he could have one of their synth modules with all the beats programmed into it. They politely laughed at him. Later, when the crew loaded up the band's trailer, Moony had some of his friends create a diversion while he nabbed the synth module, which, without a manual, he would never be able to learn how to use. The band, having discovered later that the very same piece of equipment was conspicuously missing, charged an extra thousand dollars to Moony's father's credit card and performed a song called "The Fan Who Stole Humpty's Nose."

Perry made his way to the bathroom to get out of his damp clothes. No one noticed he was gone until they all had their drinks in hand, when their muscle memory brought them to recognize the hospitality of their host. A few people looked around but, in the end, did little but catch the eyes of the others looking around.

Stephen Lloyd Webber

❖ ❖ ❖

Clicking on the Frog House bathroom's hand dryer sent Perry Whitecomb a steady blast of heat, which eroded his mind into sensations of Elysian pleasure. Moderately delusional for the sake of gratification, he entertained himself with the fantasy that numerous small kittens licked the moisture off his cold skin.

"Who's the lion in this den?" he muttered as if challenging himself, eyeing his bare backside, then the unlockable bathroom door.

He watched a soft clump of snow from his hair melt in the bright metal sink. The liquid pooled and disappeared. As he grew warmer, he felt invigorated, full of an exciting new life. He imagined himself as a great yawning cat, a creature full of comfort yet willing to devour the young of other males. He leaned back and scratched his hairy chest, moaning deeply. His skin reddened and swelled a little as his circulation restored itself. Above him, he noticed fresh water spots on the ceiling tiles he had just replaced.

"Aw, dammit," he muttered, hands finding their way onto his penis. For Perry, what followed after this discovery was unavoidable.

❖ 30 ❖

Leaving the bathroom wearing a slightly dry white shirt and wet slacks, he made himself a Long Island iced tea in a tall and slender glass.

❖ ❖ ❖

Heath dreamed peacefully about giant gorillas. On the periphery, conversations drifted and dissolved like cigarette smoke in still air:

" ... told him I wasn't paying that much for a transmission flush, and he looks at me like I just insulted his mother ..."

"... heard they're closing the Safeway on Alameda. My sister says it's because they're putting in some kind of government facility underneath ..."

"... three years in Bogotá and I never once saw a monkey. Everyone asks about monkeys ..."

"... Started putting ice in my beer. Best decision I ever made ..."

" ... she's dating some guy who works for the power company now. Says he can tell her which neighborhoods are using the most electricity at night. Weird thing to brag about, right?"

The jukebox in the corner was silent this early in the day, but everyone knew it would spring to life around happy hour, its selection of songs unchanged since 2003.

As Heath began to snore, somewhere in Deb, a switch flipped. "Have you all heard those strange noises coming from the Q block apartments?"

Josh, the lonely devout satanist who lived in the Q apartments on the second floor, perked up.

"I have," said Deb, and only Deb. "I've heard some strange noises coming from the third floor."

Moony took a swig from his beer. He was thinking about sex. In general, about how sex was great. He didn't believe other people truly understood the significance of this fact. In fact, Deb was alluding to sex in her monologue. Her interruption was timely.

"I've heard a lot of moaning, screaming, but a good sort of screaming"–she nudged Moony–"and lots of banging. I don't know if anyone heard. I am positive this noise is bothering other tenants. I myself heard the racket while I was performing some regularly-scheduled maintenance"–she paused for effect–"near the third floor." She leered at Moony as if she were telling a ghost story.

The truth was, Celia's moans during sex were not loud. They were the soothing, heart-opening, delicious exultations of a true sensate, and while a handful of tenants had heard them through the nearly hollow drywall, they were not troubled by them and, on a few occasions, were inspired to summon their loved ones and create some competitive moaning of their own.

The tenant living below Moony was Josh, who had no loved one yet was a fairly accomplished masturbator. He fantasized about Debbie Harry and listened to Blondie when he jacked off.

If there was truth in Deb's story, it was accidental. She believed her story would allude to the sex she and Celia had in Moony's bed while he was away. Deb wanted to create social tension. Many alcoholics thrive on social tension because this drives them to drink.

The scene was interrupted by the sound of scraping at the back door. No one had bothered to check it to see whether the snow had also drifted there. It had not. Some may say that wind is fickle, but it is not. Wind is merely unpredictable, and it seems especially so for those who pay very little attention to any natural forces.

Perry unlocked and opened the door, which swung outward with ease. Sunlight flooded into the bar and caused the crowd to scatter like roaches.

❖ ❖ ❖

In through the open door stomped Julio, carrying a snow shovel. He wore a tuxedo and a scarf, his hair parted with oil so thick it must have mimicked the protection from elements that ducks receive from their feathers.

When the door clanked shut behind him, everyone returned to their barstools, drinks, and conversations. "Hola," said Julio to the candlelit room. He was well aware that it annoyed both Perry and Deb to hear him speak Spanish. Though they were his bosses, he knew he did his job just well enough to avoid getting fired.

The room's momentum had dispersed somewhat after the exposure to light and what that might signify as to their duties to the outside world. Moony returned the "Hola" and curled his upper lip, trying to get his skin to feel what it was like to sport a mustache.

"I hope I am not late for the second movie," Julio whispered. Taking a moment to look around, he realized the situation, decided to have a Ballena of Pacifico, and sat next to Moony. He raised his voice so his conversation with Moony might reach the entire room. "The damnedest thing happened on Friday."

Deb recoiled at hearing the word *damnedest* as if it were a viper.

"I was minding my business cleaning the bathroom in the gym, and I found this." He whipped out a little white camera, insect-like with several antennae. "It was on the ceiling tile. Some strange cholo has been taking photographic images of people crapping in the gym bathroom, I suspect."

As is the case for any disgusting prospect not clearly sincere or sarcastic, at first, no one reacted. Celia giggled. She looked down at her drink. She was very pretty, so people took a moment before they averted their eyes.

Julio set the camera on the bar. At the *tick* of plastic on wood, people eyed it as they would alien life.

Moony squinted at the small device, supposing there were two possible scenarios here. One was the pervert scenario, of which he supposed Julio to be the most likely culprit. The other was far less likely. A bathroom was a terrible location to pick up anything meaningful, and the Sod Hill gym was never going to be among the known whereabouts of any persons of interest.

"Too bad how these civilians get so worked up about privacy," he thought. These "hardworking folks," as his father always called ordinary citizens inevitably caught in operational crossfire, were so predictably outraged at the thought of bathroom surveillance yet oblivious to how thoroughly monitored their financial lives already were.

There was the vanishingly small chance that someone was monitoring for negotiations relevant to the Ecuadorian engagement. The Chinese had locked up most of the lithium triangle, and everyone was scrambling for alternatives. The camera could be evidence there was someone watching the watchers. Looking around the room, he highly doubted that.

"Anyone need a refill?" asked Deb. She gave herself one. She was having a margarita. She decided that Celia would also have a margarita. Jon-Jon asked for a refill of his Tom Collins. Deb happily obliged.

Jon-Jon, a meth user, hence addict, paid Deb for his drink by telling her a story about the time he had forgotten to zip his fly after returning from the men's room at McDonald's when he got the Ronald clown gig there. He had gotten fired for that. Deb said that sounded terrible. Jon-Jon said that he's always been extra careful since then. Deb said, "No kidding" and returned to her conversation with Celia.

Perry sat alone at the far end of the bar, shivering like a homeless man and smelling like a wet property manager. Moony gave him his leather jacket. Perry thanked him.

"Ladies, get a load of 'em," he said, envying how easily the two women were getting along.

Jon-Jon, returning from the bathroom, paused next to the two men. "You ever hear the one about the lady and the giraffe?"

Neither of them had.

"There was this lady in Africa who was poor, so she asked her parents how she could become rich. Her parents said they weren't wise enough to be rich and that maybe her grandfather would know, since he was very old and wise."

Perry leaned close to Jon-Jon, eager to hear the joke. Moony didn't lean but looked charmed nonetheless, toying with his imaginary facial hair.

"She asked her grandfather what a classy lady like her could do for money around the village. Her grandfather didn't know because poor people couldn't think since they had to work all day. He was wiser than young people, but he wasn't wise enough to figure out how to be rich. Only rich people had the time to be wise."

Perry was chuckling already.

"So her grandfather said she should go out into the woods and ask the giraffe since the giraffe never worked a day in its life and was very tall and so could see things from a better perspective. So the girl goes and asks the giraffe."

"Giraffe, huh?" Perry said.

"The giraffe looked down at the girl like she was a tiger and backed away because he was scared."

"Uh-oh!" Perry said.

"She says in her most non-tiger voice, 'Excuse me, Mr. Giraffe, but would you please tell me how to be rich like you are?' The giraffe relaxed when he realized she was a girl, and he shook his head and said, 'I will tell you how you can become rich.' Do you want to hear what he said to her?"

"Yeah," said Perry.

"'All you have to do to get rich is become a giraffe like me! People are born into their position, and that can't be changed. But if you're lucky, you might get to be a giraffe someday.'"

At this last line, Perry completely deflated. He looked a dozen years older. Jon-Jon checked his fly to make sure it was still up, giggling exactly like Bozo would, if he had told the joke. Jon-Jon had a square of pink toilet paper sewn to the back of his jeans.

"Yeah. That's fairly accurate." Moony paused, ate a peanut.

Perry put his head in his hands. Moony noticed that his shoulders moved up and down, which signified that Perry was crying. Moony put his hand on his back.

"What the hell is wrong with this guy?" Moony often said things aloud that he didn't intend to, but things usually turned out in his favor anyway.

No one else saw Perry as he cried for the second time that day; everyone else was engaged in the story Julio was telling about the time he tried to race his best friend on horseback. Julio used to own horses. His grandfather was a rancher in Sonora. Julio, it turned out, lost the race, but his friend's horse split two of its hooves. So the way Julio figures it, he won in the long run.

"*A la larga, el que persiste gana,*" said Julio, which meant something like "In the long run, the persistent one wins." Deb glowered at him from behind the bar for his use of Spanish.

Perry wiped his eyes, shivering. "Getting back together with Deb isn't easy."

Moony nodded, though he just didn't know enough about the two of them to care.

"I keep thinking she's into you."

"She's banging Celia." Moony figured he would do what most people did when easing into things and wait until later to confess that he, too, was, on occasion, sleeping with Deb in a sexual way.

"Such a very affectionate person. I mean, look at her."

Moony took the opportunity to appraise Deb. Her blonde hair caught the candlelight from the bar. There was calculation in her glances that reminded him of his mother's friends—women who knew exactly what their looks could accomplish in a room full of men. But Moony wasn't thinking about any of that. He was thinking about how her lips parted slightly when she caught him looking.

Deb was hot. Normally that's all it would take for him to forget about his troubles and set aside his ennui. Not so now. When she turned away, he sat on his barstool and flirted with the possibility of being a no one.

Actually, he looked just like an ordinary such-and-such who sat next to some flickering candles in a rapidly cooling bar.

❖ ❖ ❖

Moony's mind went back to a moment in his apartment three months prior.

His phone rang at 2:47 a.m. He'd been deep in a game of *Zelda II*, dying repeatedly to Iron Knuckle, when the unknown number lit up his screen.

"Who is this?"

"Hello Kitty."

"Hello, Kitty."

"Moony, I need your help."

He paused the game.

"It's three in the morning. I never gave you my number."

"I'm in trouble. Real trouble. Can you come?"

Moony looked up at the screen. Link stood frozen in the Palace on the Sea, three rooms where Iron Knuckle waited. He'd spent two hours getting here—past the invisible floor maze, through the false walls, collecting enough magic to cast Jump repeatedly. The palace had no save points. If the power cut out, if he left now, he'd have to navigate the whole thing again. But Kitty's voice had a quality that made it hard for Moony to think with anything other than his dick.

Twenty minutes later, he stood outside a garden-level apartment in Capitol Hill, the kind of place where young professionals lived before they made real money. Kitty met him at the door wearing latex gloves and an expression her face wasn't designed for: genuine worry. She held a bag of frozen peas to her eye, and her mascara ran in dark streams down her face. She wore a man's white dress shirt, unbuttoned too far to be accidental, and black yoga pants that sat low on her hips. No bra–that much was obvious. Her hair, which had been perfectly styled in ringlets and spirals at Frog House, was now tied back in a simple damp-looking ponytail.

The place looked like a crime scene. Overturned furniture, broken glass, dark stains on the beige carpet that could have been wine if you lied to yourself about how they were obviously arterial blood.

Moony felt his blood chill and his body tense up. He'd been hoping this was some elaborate booty call–Kitty playing damsel, him playing hero, clothes coming off. But those stains were real. The copper smell in the air was real. Whatever had happened here was several zip codes past role-play.

He calculated: be a gentleman, help clean this up, and get more entangled in whatever this was or do the correct thing and call 911. His dick, realizing it wasn't getting anything out of this episode, voted for the correct thing.

Moony stared at the blood. "Did you call the police?"

"No! He had friends on the force. They won't help. We need to clean this up and get out of here."

"Are you OK?"

She nodded, then shook her head, then shrugged. "I just want to leave. I'm so scared."

Interesting note: she didn't seem scared.

"We need to make it look like he was never here." She gestured to kitchen gloves. "Can you help?"

Moony finally understood. She'd been on the make that night at Frog House, not some random pickup making eyes at him while he was drunk and celebrating. Something like this had been planned all along. She'd obviously wanted to get in his good graces and now was cashing out.

Which meant she would owe him.

For a guy who'd moved out to nowhere suburbia to figure out what he wanted, this could be the start of something. Help someone dispose of a crime scene, and they're yours forever.

The prospect of getting involved in something this messy didn't scare him. There was no body that he could see. They'd made it easy for him to play ignorant. That meant this was a test of trust.

❖ ❖ ❖

They worked in silence.

Moony helped roll up the stained carpet while Kitty sprayed everything with bleach.

"Of course we start with bleach," she said, then pulled out a bottle of Pine-Sol and a container of baking soda. "But we have to finish with these. It's more authentic."

Moony suspected that this was one of those times when he was in the hands of someone who didn't know what the hell they were talking about but that debating cleaning techniques would make that fact visible, and he preferred to ignore it.

For a moment, he felt like he was finally living the life his father had hinted at—the kind of work that required discretion, nerve, the ability to handle situations that would break ordinary people. This was what real operators did, wasn't it? Clean up messes, protect assets, maintain operational security.

But as he scraped dried blood from under his fingernails, reality poked in. James Bond never spent three hours on his hands and knees with a scrub brush, reeking of Pine-Sol and wondering if he was about to contract hepatitis. The glamorous world of intelligence work, it turned out, smelled like a gas station storeroom and involved a lot more manual labor than he'd imagined.

In the bathroom, he noticed flex-cuffs in the trash and what might have been a tooth near the drain. His stomach turned thinking about what Kitty had endured. Or maybe had simply inflicted on someone else.

"It's best if you don't look too close," Kitty said behind him in a sweet tone, as if they were preparing for a surprise birthday party. "Just clean."

They loaded everything into a powder-blue van with a My Child Is an Honor Student bumper sticker.

"We can't put the carpet in that dumpster," she said, pointing to one behind the building. "It faces north. Bad energy for cover-ups."

"I think we're knee deep in bad energy at this point."

"Feng shui is important in all aspects of life, moon-moon. Even cleanup."

The carpet went into an east-facing dumpster behind a construction site. By 5 a.m., they'd returned to scrub the walls and steam clean what remained.

"I can't thank you enough. For your discretion. And your help." She kissed him and moved as if to do more, but it felt forced, awful. His mind turned at once to the paused video game awaiting him back at Sod Hill.

Before he left, she stopped him. "You didn't ask any questions. That's what I told her you'd be like."

"Told who?"

"My sister's the real artist with all this. She wanted to know if you were playacting or the real thing. I said I'd find out."

In the growing dawn light, he could tell she didn't have a black eye. Her wrists and the rest of her body showed not the remotest sign of injury.

He thought about the way she'd known exactly which dumpsters had no cameras. But trauma made people prepared, he reasoned.

It wasn't until now, sitting in the candlelit bar three months later, that he wondered whose apartment they'd really cleaned, and what the hell kind of operation required a minivan with honor student bumper stickers.

❖ ❖ ❖

Moony climbed upstairs onto the roof of Frog House.

Perry decided he would have a cigarette, too, even though he had finally quit smoking months ago after an embarrassing twenty-year struggle. Moony offered him an American Spirit, assuring him with a wagging eyebrow, a wink, and an obscene pursing of the lips that since they were all natural, he could be comfortable in enjoying just this one.

Perry eyed Moony like a curious dog, sniffed at his cigarette—tobacco reminded him of when he was in high school, when he believed he was at his peak. Moony squinted further, gnawed on the inside of his mouth, and pushed out his lips like a snow shovel, he imagined, but honestly, he looked more like a primate than a tool.

The snow, wet and heavy, had drifted up against the door and would last for days. The sunlight from the evenly foggy sky was bright—Moony was unable to open his eyes more than a millimeter, and objects weren't registering much detail. Luminosity existed in place of a landscape. The streets were a memory. Snow had laid a two-foot-thick blanket over anything recognizable. White puffs had drifted into mounds so tall the world was entirely unfamiliar. The city stayed silent under its little billows. He caught the impression that there was something strong and unavoidable hidden beneath the rounded shapes made by the drifted snowfall, as if he had hidden a stone in a past life and then stumbled upon it a generation later. He couldn't see anything specific, though, so he shook off this impression.

Moony, a gentleman, lit Perry's cigarette first. He eyed a particular snowdrift that was so tall they might be able to walk right off the roof of the building without falling. Across the parking lot on the third floor of the Q complex was Moony's balcony. His collection of miniature flags from the countries he had visited were still visible, weighed down by thin sheets of clear ice. There were thirty-two of them dragging their silky rayon heads toward the ground.

The men watched, comfortable in not exchanging words. Perry thought to ask which country was the most beautiful, but he also thought better of it, since world travel might have been out of his league.

"I used to be a cop," Perry said.

Moony looked down at Perry's mustache. It looked like an alpaca was stretched out sleeping on the man's lip.

"Yeah," Perry continued. "Got into it because I wanted to make the world level and square."

Moony looked out at the mounds of rounded snow and the level-and-square domiciles that lay beneath them.

"What kind of cop?"

"Bit of everything. Small town. Booker, Texas," he said. "Population fifteen hundred, but we had a federal training facility. Strange thing for such a small place, right? But Pantex was just down the road."

Moony knew Pantex—where they assembled nuclear weapons.

"Sometimes we'd get visitors. Suits from Washington. They'd take some of our suspects for 'processing,' and we'd never see them again. I learned not to ask questions, but I can't say as I liked it much."

"It takes a certain kind."

Perry relished a long pull on his cigarette. "One time I was catching some shut-eye in my patrol car; woman out of nowhere knocked on the window. Woke me up because she wanted to do things to me out of appreciation." Perry snorted. "I later learned people do that to make a good name for themselves with the law. It's the uniform. Can't take it personal." He looked at Moony. "How's your folks?"

Someone well versed in microexpressions would have noticed that Moony was taken aback. He'd been drunk in Perry's company once or twice before, but he was sure he hadn't mentioned anything of his family to the man.

"Busy, I guess would be the right answer. They're always busy."

Perry nodded knowingly. "I know it's no comparison, but the reason why I stopped being a lawman is that it takes hold of your whole life. I'm not talking about working long hours. I'm talking about that's who you become." He paused. "I wanted to do my own thing. Like you."

Moony watched his flags, eyed Ecuador. The notion of Moony doing his own thing was certainly the image he wanted to give off, but it was anything but true. What was true? The truth of Moony was that he'd grown up learning the many ways in which other people—the people who did things in the world—were literal pawns in an overleveraged investment scheme. A few people in the world, his family among them, brokered deals and made arrangements, and everyone else got moved around to make those deals happen.

He had always wanted to believe he was a boy who did clandestine things that were not to be discussed. While other children were learning to tie shoelaces, young Daniel Adams Jr. convinced himself he was learning which shoelaces could be used to strangle someone or how to tie your laces in a way that sent a coded message. While teenagers were learning to drive, Moony told himself he was learning how to discern at a glance whether your driver could be trusted.

The thing was, nobody in the family actually talked like this. The bulk of the relationship he had with his father had been about how he should understand leveraged buyouts and debt restructuring. But somewhere along the way, Moony had started translating it all into a different language, one where "identifying vulnerabilities" meant something sexier than reading balance sheets, where "maintaining cover" was more than just not mentioning some aspects of the family business at certain parties.

He'd embarrassed them more than once. The time he'd asked his father, at a dinner with actual senators, whether a Central American project was "the operation we discussed." The way Dan Senior's face had been pained, as anyone's would be, when confronted with something stupid boldly stated. "We're just trying to get a road paved, son. That's the entire operation."

He hadn't believed him then. He still wasn't sure he believed him now. Because his father's primary instruction—repeated during hunting trips, golf games, and summer internships at various family holdings—was always the same: Look for opportunities; don't act. Let them show weakness. A person's desire for human connection was nearly always the vulnerability worth exploiting. Connection was nothing more than the basic animal desire to feel safe, he said. Sometimes this desire urged sheep to try and befriend wolves. Master that formula, and you could get whatever you wanted. So they had taught him. So he believed.

Once, after too many bourbons, his father had gotten philosophical. "You know the problem with people who work for you? They know what they're worth. Every specialist is one good offer away from becoming someone else's specialist. Loyalty is just a question of price." He'd looked at Moony strangely. "The holy grail would be someone who doesn't know what they are. Can't sell information you don't know you have. Can't betray a mission you don't remember."

"Like MKUltra?" Young Moony had read about it online—CIA mind-control experiments from the Cold War, trying to create programmable agents through drugs, trauma, and hypnosis.

Hearing him say this, his father had smiled. "That's the eternal question."

Moony had never known whether to file the memory away as drunk rambling or his father had been trying to explain to Moony that he was just such an agent. He gave Perry a knowing nod and a half smile. "I guess I'm still trying to sort out what's next for me. Give myself some space to find my muse."

Something—a bit of melting water on a sheet of ice on a white car door in the distance—shone a momentary spot of blinding white at Moony's dull brown eyes. He squinted, and it was gone. And then he said something he himself didn't understand: "I wonder why freedom lands most readily in the laps of those who would just as well trade it for something else—a villa on Lake Como or a few more percentage points in their investments."

He looked over at Perry. "Guys like you actually know what to do with more freedom, and you deserve to have it."

Perry grunted in manful approval.

❖ ❖ ❖

Perry and Moony returned inside, down the sewer-smelling spiral staircase to the sound of Celia and Deb each singing a different song at once. Citrus light-flecks from candles danced over their faces, and people at the bar laughed raucously. Behind them, paper cutouts of cartoon happy faces swung lazily on a string like fluorescent shrubbery in an aquarium.

Moony sat at a table by himself and watched Heath breathe. Heath, asleep, possessed a sort of peace he could not identify. The Swede's velvet pullover made him look like Little Red Riding Hood with the build of an itchy running back.

Julio marched over to Moony, grabbed his wrist, put the miniature camera in his hand, and accused him of being the one who planted it in the gym's bathroom. Moony was miles away from doing any such thing, but Julio, a man who had a very long, very narrow mustache, didn't seem to hear, and all everyone else was doing was laughing, drinking, and threatening Moony with the evidence that he was a massive pervert.

As the man who looked like God mentioned, perhaps it was Julio who placed the camera there.

"I say there was no camera at all," said the man who nursed Bud Light from a can. "I never seen a camera in a bathroom before."

"Hand over the photographs," said another man.

Julio dragged Moony toward the bathroom of the bar, commanding that since Moony was depraved, he therefore hid cameras everywhere he went—if there was a hidden camera in Frog House's bathroom, it would prove Moony was the one they were all after. Perry, his eyes fighting to make out solid objects in the dark bar, wagged his finger in Julio's general direction like the sheriff in an Old West movie. "God damn it, Moony is right. He didn't do anything. You let go of him right now, or I'll bust your ass!"

Julio let go of Moony only to slap his thigh and point and laugh at Perry. Moony grabbed Julio's collar and intended to dink his face against the counter. When he heard the meaty thunk resound, he realized he had been too forceful. The merriment around the bar subsided—a little.

Moony said he was sorry, and scratched the back of his own curly-haired head. He tried to feel Julio's pain. Deb set down her drink and hopped onto the counter, leaning over in front of Moony to check on Julio. She was generous with the view down her blouse. Julio would have a multicolored bruise on his forehead tomorrow, but for the sake of the crowd, he pounded his fist on the counter and demanded another Pacifico.

Deb obliged.

The crowd cheered.

❖ ❖ ❖

Moony sat down between Julio and Josh. Josh's incessant talk about satanism and the necessity of blind egotism wore on everyone's nerves except his own, which pleased him, but because he got what he wanted in the short term, he could develop into nothing more than the lonely owner of a 1950 hearse who worked as a telephone support technician at a twenty-four-hour satellite television call center. He had wanted to work at a graveyard but struck out and instead was greeted each morning by the faces of those who worked the graveyard shift.

Josh's budget gothic mode of transportation got on everyone's nerves, especially those who lived near him, since every morning at six o'clock when he left for work, he fought the uphill battle to start his car. The hearse's routine was to backfire seven times, and then the alternator belt would scream until he sharply revved the engine up to 4,000 rpm. This led the car to produce a riot's worth of noise on account of his two dead cylinders, dual exhaust, and no mufflers.

The power came back on at Frog House. It took four seconds for anyone to react.

"Thank God!" said Deb, and held up her drink, which was now a Coors Light, to salute God, apparently.

Stephen Lloyd Webber

The man who looked like God gave a dignified cheer.

Julio charged over to the front door as if carrying heavy bags, intending to make an exit where he said "See you later, suckers." He made the incorrect assumption that since the power returned, the snow would no longer be packed up against the front door. He yipped for help as mountains of white cascaded onto him.

Remembering his previous situation, Perry grinned toward Moony, who was also being smiled at by Celia. Moony chose Celia.

She gave him a suggestive look that was so lazily sexy only she could pull it off. She was a paid professional face model. Though her boyfriend believed her when she talked about her days attending class at college, she was eighteen and spent her days pursuing her budding career baring her olive skin at modeling gigs. He didn't know how old she was, but he wouldn't have had any qualms about their age difference.

He grabbed his coat and, on his way out the back door, nodded a stately goodbye to Perry, who realized it was already two in the afternoon, and he had another art movie to screen.

Many people in the room, including the Little Red Riding Hood asleep in the corner, had still not seen the new *King Kong*.

❖ ❖ ❖

The following day, it was pretty much true that Moony was snowed in.

A white bag of garbage sat in his kitchen next to the trash can like a sad bride at the altar, its handles tied in a bow. The bag was ready for its one and only trip to the dumpster, but there was no sign of it going anywhere. It wasn't going anywhere because Moony was the one in charge of it getting there. Moony figured that because of the weather, he would take a snow day, which for him meant taking a break from everything. A part of him really believed this was what people out in the world did.

Somehow, though, despite the weather, a woman in a bronze-and-brown polyester jumpsuit had managed to arrive at his apartment. She knocked on his door and he let her in–that was how that went.

He recognized her as the strange woman who'd called herself the Gypsy, the older sister of the woman who smelled like cedar.

Anyone who knew the Gypsy understood that she lived her life in a miasma of altered perceptions; she had taken so many mind-manifesting chemicals in coordination with each other, her personal sphere had dissolved. The world she moved around in was one of spirits and glowing energies. She had graduated beyond guinea pig to become something of an authority figure on psychoactive living.

Moony welcomed her in without much thought as to why she might drop by or what he might offer as a means of explaining her presence to Celia. He was the sort of person who always gave room to others to explain their own existence. Some grant space out of courtesy; he did so now to relieve himself of the burden of responsibility.

The Gypsy also said nothing. She made herself welcome by sitting on his leather sofa and pulling out a wooden box. Opening it, Moony could see it was filled with cash. She began counting the money and looked satisfied—her cracked and busy hands were given a purpose.

"Do you ever lose time?" she asked casually.

"What?"

"Hours you can't account for. Gaps."

Moony thought about it. "Doesn't everyone?"

"Not like I mean." But she didn't elaborate. She took her time counting money, enjoying noticing quantities rise. "Calamine double alpha," she said quietly, watching his face.

Moony looked at her.

"Sigmoid November threshold." She kept counting, looking at him to catch his reaction. Nothing registered in his expression. Moony couldn't find the remote, so he groaned and walked over to switch on the floor lamp by hand. Eyes flashed up to him as he moved, then back down to the stack of bills. The Gypsy was high strung.

In the bedroom, Celia slept like one of the logs that waited indefinitely for the fireplace. She always denied that she snored, but sure enough, she snored, happy under a thick comforter. The bedroom's TV played the end scene from *King Kong*.

"Your father had interesting ideas about personnel management," she said.

"I never worked for him."

"No."

She kept counting. "But he invested in you. Curious to see if it took."

Moony shrugged. "He always said the best returns come from investments you forget about."

She stopped counting entirely, looked at him. "Did he now?"

"Something like that." Moony found a nearly empty pack of American Spirits wedged between couch cushions.

"Your father's company has contracts in places that keep having convenient regime changes. Your sister was in Montana—rare earth territory, Chinese competition." She didn't look up when she spoke. "Was she like you?"

Moony's jaw tightened at the use of past tense referring to his sister. He recognized the depiction of a few Eastern Orthodox saints on the silver rings on the Gypsy's fingers.

"The way you helped my sister clean. You asked no questions. You knew exactly what to do. Someone invested serious training in you. She called me to the bar because she said you had dropped a line about 'family operations.' About 'clearance levels.'"

He tried to remember what he'd said that night. He'd been drunk. Probably showing off.

"She said you read like someone trained."

"I played sports in school. I was OK." He made his expression serious. "I had to be."

She stopped counting and stood to face him.

"I'm going to tell you something, and I want you to listen carefully. I've done this with many people. Most of them know things. They know things because someone taught them or because they stumbled into knowing. And when I ask the right question, I can see it. The little flinch."

She came around to face him.

"You don't flinch. You don't know anything. You're just a boy who learned some words."

He wanted to argue, but she wasn't wrong.

"But," she continued, and something shifted in her face—not warmer, but more practical—"a boy who learned some words can still be useful. Can still hold a deed. Can still sign where he's told to sign. The question is whether you're going to be difficult about it."

She pointed at the money.

"Here's the sum you need to pay the keeper of the threshold," she said. "First installment. Proof of concept."

Moony guessed the sum was around $250,000. "Keeper of the threshold? Sounds like a job with a lot of entry-level requirements."

She waited for him to make a move.

He made no move.

"Your father equips you for one thing, then lets you park here like a car in long-term storage," she said.

He didn't like how hard the statement hit him. "Proof of what concept?"

"That there are other games besides the one your family plays. Better games."

"I'm listening."

"My interests have been putting some of their money into American real estate. Properties nobody asks questions about. The government can't track who owns what—not really. Not when it's done properly." She paused, studying his reaction. "These properties serve dual purposes. Clean money, yes. But also—"

"Listening posts," Moony finished, trying to sound knowing. "Safe houses."

The Gypsy smiled but looked altogether bored. "The world is full of such enlightened commerce, free from outside control. Your family plays in a league beyond me, but these are not times to be big."

She wasn't wrong. The old arrangements his father had with various government contacts—they'd only become greater liabilities as things got more transparent.

"You're talking about me setting up a parallel network," he said. "Keeping my family in the dark."

"Your father's people won't realize what you're building until it's too late to stop."

This sounded exactly like the kind of work his father had always hinted he'd be ready for someday—building networks, managing assets, playing the great game. Finally, someone was offering him a chance to prove he understood what the family business was really about. The old man would be livid if he followed through with it, because of how thoroughly it would cock up his real identity. But if Moony was able to make it work, he'd earn his father's approval for taking initiative like this, and it would mean he'd become something to be feared in his own right —no longer just the Adams heir, a beneficiary of old contracts, but a player himself, if only a minor one.

The alternative was to refuse, to muster up the cajónes to call the old man and convince him he was good enough to be looped in on Ecuador.

"Americans don't pay attention to who owns what. Takes too much real work. Perfect for people who need to park money quietly."

"And you want me to help your Russian friends."

She wrinkled her nose and shot him a look as if he'd passed gas, and a lungful of it had hit her nostrils in full force. "You know this isn't about countries.

"The money," she continued, "it's for your first property. Aurora AAAA Storage. Insanely boring, not profitable, perfect for our needs. I'll have someone discuss with you about what comes after once a few more pieces are in place."

"And if I say no?"

"Then you'll see someone else win instead of you. Once you see the details, you'll understand why. I appreciate what you did to help Kitty, and I trust you won't disappoint us here. The keeper of the threshold will advise you as to next steps."

"What if you're wrong about me, and I'm just a trust fund douche playing video games?"

"My dear, I understand perfectly well that's exactly what you are." She moved toward the door. "But that won't stop you from buying exactly what I need you to buy, and you'll do it properly because you were trained to understand. Even if you don't remember learning it."

❖ ❖ ❖

She'd made her offer, and that was that.

He stared for a while at the indifferent figure she cut walking away from him, feeling something gurgle and shift in his understanding. "Even if you don't remember learning it."

It felt thrilling. Had his entire childhood actually been some kind of slow-burn training program? Each piece seemingly normal for someone of his background, but the accumulation . . .

He remembered Yvette asking him once why their family was so weird about phones. Why they had "house phones" and "other phones." Why their father made them memorize numbers instead of saving them. "Operational security," he'd joked, but nobody laughed.

The thing was, he'd always felt like he was playing at being a spy. Like he was pretending to be Jason Bourne while actually just being a rich kid with too much time. But what if the feeling was real, and the dismissal of it was the lie he'd told himself? What if he had been shaped into something?

No wonder he felt so comfortable at Sod Hill doing nothing. He'd been trained to wait. To be ready without knowing what for. To maintain cover even when there was no operation.

The Gypsy had seen it immediately. Whatever he was, she recognized it. And now she was offering him the chance to find out if his training was real by actually using it.

He put on his Denver Broncos cap and went onto the balcony to either get fresh air or smoke a cigarette—he would decide when the time came and bring his lighter in case.

Outside, surrounded by the collection of souvenir flags he'd hung from the railing, Moony saw that the storm had blown Portugal off the edge.

"Bye bye, Portugal," he said, cigarette dangling precariously from his lip. He straightened the remaining flags, wondering if the cold numbness in his hands was what death felt like. He exhaled deeply, satisfied at how breath plumed like smoke to join the clouds. For a while, he pretend-smoked. Then he lit his cigarette, making it halfway through before getting bored with it and cold and unsettled in himself, certain that going inside was all he needed to calm his system.

He thought of Celia as a napping baby he was being quiet for and slid the balcony door open, returning inside to reread the email his mother had sent a few weeks before, placing himself in the past before he had learned of Yvette's death.

Dan,

Is Yvette with you? I haven't heard from her.

Mom

Dan was his father's name. Dan Jr. was Moony's unofficial name—he hadn't gone by it since he was nine, when his grandfather first began telling stories of the horse named Moony he liked to ride. Each time Thurman Jr. told the tale, he mistook certain details. What began as a story of Dan riding a horse named Moony became the tale of the nine year-old Adams boy who practiced night and day riding a horse named Dan, even though his mother did not allow it. He would laugh, and everyone around would indulge him, when in fact it was Thurman's son, Dan Senior, who discouraged horse riding, though he was seldom present enough to enforce his demand that his son "do something less expensive."

The way Thurman Jr. told the story had Moony eventually winning a trophy for some aspect of horsemanship. Moony couldn't recall doing this and often wondered where the trophy had gone. The Adams side of his family indulged the notion, and Dan received the nickname Moony.

Moony had written his mother back a note that demonstrated ignorance, hence innocence, as to his sister's whereabouts. There was a bitter irony in the fact that an organization capable of tracking financial transactions and mining supply chains across continents couldn't keep tabs on its own family members. If his mother didn't know what Yvette had done, Moony wouldn't be the one who interfered with her ignorance. He chose instead to deflect the situation to his younger brother Alex, whom he suspected was working his way through the very Montana operation where Yvette had met her end.

I'll bet you a million bucks Alex is in her neck of the woods. If not, swing by and collect your bucks. That kid. How inconsiderate.

Dan

When Moony (Daddy-Pops) had received the phone call from the Montana police informing him of Yvette's death, he gave the authorities his mother's and father's phone numbers and called his father. When no one answered, he left a message and flushed his phone down the toilet bowl.

After another few minutes of numbing out to the Gypsy's proposition and some habitual rumination on his dead sister,

Moony figured it was high time for him to hose down his attentional palate.

He went across the hall to see what his neighbor was up to.

❖ ❖ ❖

Heath answered the door at the second knock. He looked pure, like he had just seen the face of God in a shiny surface.

He had.

He had gazed at the underside of a stainless steel cook pot until the creator of the universe stared back at him, wondering what he wanted from him. Heath just wanted to say hello. God understood, as God always did.

Heath cradled the God pot in his arms like a baby. Shadrack kicked a soccer ball into a burgundy handbag goal.

Heath, eyes wide and face tranquil, said nothing and stepped mindfully into Moony's apartment. His bare feet looked like a seventy-year-old man's. Moony closed the door to his bedroom, where Celia lay snoozing.

"I hope you don't mind if I have a seat," Heath said, sitting down. This would not be the last time Heath sat down in Moony's apartment. You will be told when it is.

Moony asked Heath how it was going, wondering if his neighbor was imagining he could crawl headfirst inside the cook pot, *Trainspotting* style. In that moment, Moony realized what he admired about him: here was a person not intending to be anything besides whatever he happened to be.

As dissimilar as Heath was from Perry, Moony saw something similar in both men, an unselfconsciousness somewhere in the psyche that Moony himself had been trained to obliterate. To be so aware of one's effects on others and how each gesture might cause ripples in power dynamics or result in favorable circumstances.

There was a knock at the door. Female knuckles.

Moony opened the door. Deb, his landlord, so wide eyed as to inadvertently appear sad, wearing a white fur coat over a white tank top, leaned close to Moony's face, smelling like mint toothpaste.

"Busy?"

Moony stepped aside, gesturing to her that of course her presence was welcome.

Heath stared down at the cook pot with a wide boyish smile.

Deb said, "Yum" regarding the stacks of bills on Moony's coffee table, draped her fur coat on his couch, and made herself comfortable. She made Moony uncomfortable in a certain way.

Heath did not acknowledge Deb, who, in the current low light, resembled a bleach-blonde virgin Mary; God the father was in the cook pot, packing his dirty laundry into a Kenmore washing unit from 1977. He was washing jeans and whistling something Heath couldn't hear. He could only get a visual from the cook pot.

"There is a fair amount of incriminating evidence here." Deb kicked her shoes onto the floor like she owned the place.

"I guess so," Moony said, wondering if she wanted to be paid off or something.

"You left your watch at my place," she said, producing Moony's missing watch.

"I've never been to your place."

Deb winked at him. In a movement of body and hands as graceful as sliding off a bracelet, she produced a vintage Polaroid camera from a sort of holster. It had a leather body and chrome accents. She set it atop the stacks of cash, leaned back into the chair, and let her legs part open. "I've been documenting all the beautiful moments around here," she said, her fingers tracing up her thigh. "You'd be surprised what develops."

Moony tried hard to imagine this going in any direction but the one he himself would envision.

The bedroom door opened and Celia walked out, rubbing her eyes. She was stark naked, all right.

In a hurry to remedy the situation, Moony raced to her and wrangled her into the bedroom. She had a flashback of sexual abuse from one of her foster dads, but then she recognized her Moony-O. He half tossed her onto the bed, and, as it goes, she half flew herself onto the bed. It was a delicate bounce she received from the bedsprings. She started kissing him, so naturally he kissed back.

Deb made herself present in the bedroom doorway, and she liked what she saw.

Off came Moony's clothes.

Deb applied fresh lip gloss and crawled into bed.

Heath, cradling the pot, stood in the bedroom doorway and nodded with the rightness of all situations. His heart was glad that the three on the bed seemed to be getting along as well as anything in the world. Then he turned and went into Moony's kitchen. He was hungry, he decided. Maybe there was something for him in one of the cabinets. Plus, he didn't want to talk to anyone right now. Telling anyone about his revelation would only diminish the experience, and no one would believe him.

The two ladies in bed did not encourage Moony to think very deeply about anything else at the moment, so he didn't.

❖ ❖ ❖

Heath was walking around Moony's kitchen carrying a bag of croissants in one hand and the God pot in the other when he heard what he believed to be actual voices.

He ambled over into the living room and peered around to detect the source of the audibly emitted phonemes. Realizing they were coming from beyond the front door in the hallway, he set down the pot on Moony's coffee table, hearing but not understanding snippets of Russian:

"Ты готов к этому?" (Are you ready for this?)

"Да, но нужно быть осторожным." (Yes, but we need to be careful.)

He recognized the Gypsy's voice speaking to Shadrack. Heath produced the cook pot's lid and grasped it with both hands, wielding it like a shield as he tried to make out more of their conversation. Despite his efforts, the words remained in Russian. He couldn't understand a damn thing they were saying.

He swung open the door and spoke to the voices in the hallway. "Whatever you're telling him, I suppose you'll tell me, too, later?"

From the bedroom, Celia heard the commotion and got up to look, her face bright with curiosity. She had every appearance of believing that what she overheard was the preparation for some sort of jubilance. Moony's and Deb's bodies moving gently over each other on the bed behind her, she peered around the doorframe.

Shocked at Heath's presence in the apartment and their open front door, she made a small noise of outrage. It sounded like a rubber duck.

From the hallway, Shadrack kicked a soccer ball toward the source of noise. Heath, focused on phenomena neither physical nor actual, didn't seem concerned in the least about the ball's approach through the air.

The ball whizzed by his head and hit Celia square in the face. She ran back into the bedroom.

This spurred Moony to action. He leaped out of the room ready to make a mess of someone. Seeing Heath, he grabbed him by the neck and in moments had thrown him onto the floor. He sat on his chest and used both hands to pin him down. Yes, of course he was still naked.

Moony and Heath stared into each other's eyes, each hoping for a manly understanding of the situation.

"Какого хуя вы там делаете, придурки? Отдай мой мяч!" (What the fuck are you doing in there, assholes? Give me my ball!) Shadrack's voice came from the hallway. He ran into the apartment to grab the ball, tracking clumps of muddy snow across the carpet.

"Stay the fuck out of my apartment, сука блядь!" Moony yelled. It felt good to yell. But Shadrack had already nabbed the ball, and he was bouncing it with deliberate insolence.

Moony let go of Heath, realizing his Swedish neighbor had been innocent of the situation, and helped him to his feet.

Without warning, Shadrack launched into a jump kick at Moony's head. Moony caught the man's leg midair and for a moment considered applying his body weight to torque the knee perpendicular to its hinge, a move that would be excruciatingly painful and result in permanent damage. It would also necessitate a hospital trip and probably a police statement. So instead, he simply let go. The thunk of Shadrack falling to the carpet was enough to take the fight out of him.

The fall had caused a pocket knife to slip from the amphetamine connoisseur's pocket.

"Hey, that's mine," Heath said, grabbing it.

From the doorway, the Gypsy watched the scene. Celia dabbed a moist hand towel on her eye. She was comfortable in her nakedness. Shadrack was comfortable with the realization that his ball had her in the eye. He tried to shoot her a blank look that asserted a superior sense of peace with himself and left.

"See you next week," the Gypsy said to Moony.

He looked up at the woman as she turned to leave. There were two worlds here, he realized—one where a person could be wild, inconsequential, and free and another represented by this oligarch's partner where agendas were more real than the people who served them. He was sleepwalking between both worlds and belonged to neither.

It dawned on him that he loathed what she represented. Not the dirty money or the operations, but the assumption that he was already hers, that his training made him someone's pawn. But where did her agenda stop and he begin? Every instinct he had— was that him or his father's programming?

Heath's brain was busy running calculations of his own. He took in the scene and worked to do the steady arithmetic to understand all that had happened: the voices, the soccer ball,

Celia's eye, the naked wrestling match, the patterns of snow on the floor, his recovered knife. He returned to his apartment with his pot lid.

He allowed all phenomena to remain in place without totaling the sums into something tidier.

◆ ◆ ◆

Deb crawled back into Moony's bed. She wanted it to be her bed, if only for a while.

"You have some strange friends," she said. She paused. "I was talking about Celia here. Come here, sweetie."

Celia obliged.

Deb cooed in regard to Celia's wounded eye. "People are going to think you did this to her," she said to Moony.

"That sounds like a threat," he responded, crawling back into bed. He knew it was not a threat, but he didn't know why he knew.

His front door opened again.

"Hello?" It was Perry's voice. Just the nonthreatening person he didn't want to see.

Moony got out of bed. His voice cracked. "Hey, Perry."

"All right if I come in?"

"Well, I just woke up . . ."

Perry sat down on the couch, looking at the stainless steel cook pot, the camera, the stacks of cash. He shouted again at his friend in the bedroom: "Been doing some cooking? Christ, this smells like battery acid."

"In a manner of speaking," Moony said, wondering where to start as he walked into his living room, putting on an expensive T-shirt.

Perry looked down at his hand where there was once a wedding band. "I think she and I are going to get back together."

Moony wondered if Deb could hear Perry or if that would change anything. Slapping sounds came from the bedroom.

"It's great, the way this weather keeps happening."

"Things are looking bright between us. We've arrived at an agreement. I think I've come to understand what romance is. Finally, after all these years."

"Can you believe it? So much snow."

"She said she would be checking on your window—that your bedroom window had a slit she needed to look at."

"Yes. She did come by, actually."

"When?"

"You guys are swell landlords for taking care of it so quickly."

Deb, half dressed in Celia's clothes, half dressed in Moony's, but still somehow not fully dressed, walked over to Perry.

From the bedroom, the slapping sounds continued. She gave him a great big hug. "Ooh, you smell nice," Perry said.

Moony pulled his face into a tight smile as one might picture Abraham Lincoln's to be.

❖ ❖ ❖

Deb sat on Perry's lap. "Oh, baby. I am the happiest lady in the world."

Perry beamed a little nervously. "Let's hold off on the public display of affection until later."

"Moony has done a marvelous job decorating the place, don't you think?" She hopped up and down a little, rocked back and forth on Perry.

"Sure is nice." Perry gave a deep sigh. Deb continued rocking.

"The bedroom is beautiful, too. I was in there for a while, working, working away. Just working, thinking, *What a job this guy has done with the place. He can really squeeze a lot of love in between these walls.*"

"Oh yeah, that's right."

Deb watched Moony. "Sorry I took so long. Once a girl gets stuck in Moony's bedroom, well, getting out isn't easy."

"Quite true," said Perry.

"Moony is a pleasure," she said, quickly showing her teeth.

"You betcha," Perry said, reaching over to run his hand across Deb's fur coat.

Celia peeked around the corner. Naked—no one would mind.

"Uh-oh!" said Perry, noticing nudity.

"Sweetie! Come have a seat," said Deb, patting the couch very near to Perry.

"Nope." Celia, a scared mouse, zipped back into the bedroom.

"So you two—just friends, huh?" said Perry, full of winks.

"Yeah, we barely know each other," said Moony, watching Deb twirl the hair of Perry's beard.

Celia came into the living room wearing one of Moony's designer work-style shirts.

"Oh, you poor little thing! Look at that eye," said Deb.

"Ooh," said Perry. "Who did that to you?" Sure enough, he eyed Moony.

"Soccer ball injury," said Moony as she drifted to him, kissing him for considerably longer than was logical when a person has guests over.

"Racquetball," Perry repeated incorrectly. From the look on his face, something about the sound of the word he just said seemed to appeal to him. He waited for the kiss to end.

"Soccer, actually," Moony corrected.

"Moony, do you want to play racquetball tomorrow?"

Deb chimed in. "Oh, Bucko, we were going to dinner tomorrow after work."

Celia pulled away from kissing Moony and did some of her yoga right there in the living room. As she moved into downward-facing dog pose, the work shirt slipped up around her neck. She was not a person who reserved space on their list of priorities for keeping their body to themselves.

"We could play racquetball on Thursday, if you already have plans," Moony said.

Celia moved into dragon pose.

"You and me, huh, Moony?" Perry smiled.

Deb whispered something in Perry's ear. Perry decided they had better go.

Only Celia's yoga and Moony remained.

❖ ❖ ❖

Instead of playing racquetball, Perry decided that they could take a trip to Mexico. Lately, he had been full of good ideas.

Most of the snow had melted off the roads, and while cleaning up trash outside the apartment complex's mailboxes, mostly junk mail that the residents discarded as soon as they'd set eyes on it, he chanced upon a flyer advertising Puerto Peñasco as a safe and inexpensive vacation spot and decided to go for it.

He had gotten Sod Hill's business affairs in order to such an extent that if he missed two days, he could still return in time to convert Frog House into amphitheater mode for his next biweekly art film screening. He loved the theme of comparisons above all else, so he was thinking of showing two Al Pacino movies back to back, with coffee in between: *Serpico*, then *Simone*.

Though he had budgeted his time this weekend to install a European-style cappuccino maker, since art types enjoyed that sort of thing, it could wait until next week. His life would benefit instead from an open-ended vacation; he would invite his new friend Moony.

Moony was down for a Mexico trip. He didn't understand Perry's apologies regarding short notice. They dropped what they were doing, borrowed Moony's uncle's RV, and left.

On the road, they talked about Perry's groundbreaking art film idea, planning a few discussion questions to take place after them, and even brainstormed some advertisements to create a buzz. If things went well, the bar could eventually separate into an Italian section and an American section. In the Italian section, there would be a cappuccino maker and some pastries, and the rest of the bar would be pretty much the same, since it was already American.

Perry realized he didn't have to run this idea by Deb since she would just say, "Go for it, Bucko, if we can afford it," adjust her reading glasses, and get back to her paperwork.

Perry drove; Moony sat watching the scenery change. The snowdrifts shrank as they moved south, revealing the Sangre de Cristo range—sharp and looming. Then the mountains were gone, too, and the view bored him: grassland and desert.

"Looks just like the Wild West, don't it?" asked Perry.

Moony nodded. The grassland scenery looked like something he'd seen on an old television—it looked drowsy, the way antenna reception wavered when whipped by a storm. Occasionally, his mind's eye caught the image of the Gypsy's wooden money box on the coffee table, and he imagined the road noise was the feel of it in his hands, opening the box to pocket the acrid-smelling bills.

Here in Perry's presence, he was back to being in full trust fund layabout mode. He found he just couldn't take any of that Gypsy stuff seriously. He regarded the memory from the standpoint of an average human and concluded it had been a very strange thing for her to do. How preposterous it was that a near stranger had come to his house to count a stack of money and then leave it behind. He thought about how most people might fantasize hiring a detective to get to the bottom of it all. He imagined holding a monocle or a magnifying glass.

It started raining outside, and this became their only noise.

The RV was in between customization work. There was no stereo; there was no toilet—the two men used a Hills Bros. coffee can to piss in. It sat on the floor where the toilet was supposed to be and, whenever the Fleetline hit a bump, sloshed room-temperature urine onto the linoleum.

There was no bed—Moony's uncle wanted to have bunk beds since he could not tolerate sleeping next to his wife's tosses and turns, which she did because she could not abide by his snoring—so Moony and Perry didn't sleep. They used amphetamines and shared childhood stories and came to respect each other, despite their economic differences.

Moony learned that for seventy years, the Whitecomb family had been the proudest beekeepers in the state of Colorado, but Perry had never gotten over his childhood fear of bees. "Christ, I'm scared of bees," he said.

It turned out Moony was afraid of bees, too. "And I've never even been stung by a bee. My sister was stung by a wasp when she was a kid. I saw her throat swell up, and she cried like a sick monkey. I didn't know what to do. One of our housekeepers put tobacco on the sting, and we rushed her to the hospital. Do you believe in omens?"

"Not even a little."

"Yeah, I was just wondering."

Perry shared his bee sting story: "The first time my parents showed me what's what on a bee farm, I was stung by fifteen, twenty"—he looked at Moony—"maybe thirty..."

Moony gaped.

"Fifty-some bees. I swore off beekeeping. Best decision I ever made. Sixty, seventy bee stings can really whip the shit out of you."

"Is that where you got the bumps on your cheeks, from all the stings?"

"What bumps?" Perry leaned to find the rearview mirror, but there wasn't one. He swerved the RV back into the right lane.

"Christ, this steering is too tight."

Having no radio but desiring noise, Moony learned that Perry believed himself to be a man who delegated his pursuits in the desired proportions—his job, which he put his heart into, made him happy enough, and his spare time gave him satisfaction. He said he didn't believe in hobbies and that, instead, a man should follow his heart with new and challenging projects but never take himself too seriously. He said he was an open-minded fellow who had everything he wanted except children, but that, too, was all right because having everything you wanted meant less room to strive.

Perry's sunglasses were artsy, Perry thought, since they existed as very small pink circles. The man had squinty eyes, but the glasses were clearly not intended for use when driving into the Arizona sun. He realized this at one of their frequent stops for fuel, looking in the side mirror and noticing a striking redness on the whites of his eyes.

Crossing the border was effortless, but like Moony said, "It's the coming back that's the trick."

Perry had already checked that they had all the proper paperwork and none of the amphetamines in the glove box to ensure a smooth return.

When they arrived at Puerto Peñasco, both men were charmed at the number of fellow RVs and American citizens present. The two had arrived in the biggest and newest RV of them all, Perry noted. Viewed from the outside, the Fleetline recreational vehicle looked truly top of the line, an unequivocal prototype of high-stakes relaxation. Stepping outside it for the first time south of the border, Moony and Perry regarded the massive RV with drowsy awe—it had taken them from Denver to Puerto Peñasco in a single day.

The sun shone as it always did on the shores of the Sea of Cortez—gloriously, with a vibrating yellow attrition. The two men parked themselves a little way down on the beach in lawn chairs, facing the sunset.

After many beers and another bee story, Perry told Moony more about his pioneering idea to split Frog House into two sections. "One would be active during the day and one during the night. Just like different time zones. Pastries and coffee versus vodka and beer."

Moony played along. "Hmm. Well, it would mean more business all day long. Not a bad idea. There isn't a pastry shop anywhere in the neighborhood. I'd go there."

And he would, because he liked eating pastries. Perhaps he would begin waking up early enough to eat freshly made ones.

❖ ❖ ❖

In lawn chairs, the conversation made its way onto the topic of relationships. Moony noticed Perry had an erection, clearly visible through his white linen slacks. Moony attempted to keep his eyes on the loose half-moons of skin beneath Perry's eyes. He tried to get himself to chuckle inwardly, to better hear the words coming out of Perry's mouth as the man spoke, but something about the uprising and extension of that simple male cylinder there on the other side of a thin drape of cloth he found hard to disregard. Perry's plastic chair was on the back two legs, precariously balanced and bowing under the weight of a carefree man. Perry seemed to be forming some sort of meaning with his words, and strung together in phrases, they amounted to something to the effect of "Committing to a relationship is never smooth if there's other people involved. But it looks so easy from the outside."

Moony hesitated a second. "Yeah, no, absolutely, you're right," he said emphatically. He didn't know what the hell Perry was talking about.

Moments passed. The Sea of Cortez stretched before them like hammered copper in the dying light. The amphetamines had left both men with the illusion of clarity that comes from being too awake for too long—every grain of sand had been individually placed; every sound arrived with its own echo. Above them, pelicans wheeled in prehistoric formations.

Moony needed to fill the silence. "We all have things we want," he said. "The biggest lie out there is that anything is fair. We're all entitled assholes; we're all wounded assholes; we're all disadvantaged assholes. Each in our own proportions. But life is about getting what you want. Nobody keeps score."

"All right then, Dr. Psychology. Riddle me this: What if you're interested in someone, but you can't be sure whether they have a partner? Maybe they're cheating, but you don't know. Should you get into the thing?"

Lucky to have a reflexive answer, Moony gave his expert opinion: "You start to get an instinct for those things."

"And you just do 'er anyway?" Perry asked, shaking his head as if to music Moony could not hear.

"You would, too," Moony said, wondering whether his words were slurred from all the beer.

Perry rocked up and down, flexing the firm plastic legs a little. "You know what I can't figure out about you?"

"What's that?"

"You show up at Sod Hill with your fancy car and designer everything. Old-money kid, obviously. But then you're out there picking up trash, talking to me about my big dreams like you actually give a shit." Perry took a long pull from his beer. "Most rich kids I've known, they play at being poor for about a week before they get bored."

Moony shrugged. "Maybe I'm just really committed to the bit."

"See, that's what I mean. Everything's a joke to you. A bit. Like we're all just"—Perry waved his hand vaguely—"entertainment."

Moony had a point to make about Sega Genesis being a better form of entertainment, but it took him too long to order his thoughts, and by that time, Perry had continued.

"And then there's Deb." Perry's voice got louder. "I know about you two. Hell, everyone knows. What I can't figure out is why you need both her and Celia. What kind of man does that?"

Something bitter and hardwired in Moony's psyche clicked into place. "What kind of man gets turned on thinking about how much he's being taken advantage of? Anyway, Deb's her own woman. She comes and goes as she pleases. She's into Celia, and they're kind enough to loop me in when I'm around."

"Sometimes I watch you at the screenings, the way you look at people. You get this expression like you're taking notes. Like you see us, but you don't see us." Perry let his chair fall forward with a thunk. "We're not your fucking lab rats, Moony. We're real people with real lives."

"Could've fooled me."

"From where I'm sitting, I see an Adams heir who's out here playing poor after something went wrong at home. What happened up there in the big house? What happened—did Daddy's empire finally claim a casualty too close to home? And here you are, convincing yourself you're living some spy novel instead of just running away."

Moony hadn't realized Perry actually understood his situation. Perry was the first person to call him on his shit.

"You're drunk," Moony said.

"And you're slumming," Perry shot back. "Question is, why are you being such a good friend to me if, in a few months, you'll cast everything aside and move on to your next adventure?"

"Perry, this is the first real stretch of time we've spent together."

"You can belittle. It doesn't make any difference. I think you'd be a good person if you stopped being such a piece of shit. Why are you such a piece of shit?"

"You'll have to give me a few minutes if you expect me to figure that one out."

The waves crashed closer to shore as the tide came in. Moony watched the foam reach for their chairs, then retreat. Perry's breathing had gotten heavier, and when Moony glanced over, he saw his friend's face had gone red as if they had been sitting too close to a campfire. They had no campfire.

"You want to know the truth?" Perry said. "Sometimes I look at you, and I see everything I could've been if I'd been born different. If I'd had your chances." He stood up abruptly, swaying slightly. The chair tipped backward into the sand. "But then I think, *Would I even want that?* To go through life never knowing if anyone actually likes me or just wants something from me?" He laughed, but it came out bitter.

Moony noticed Perry had maintained his erection, more or less. Good for Perry. The conversation had taken such a turn that this member's continued presence now seemed of a piece with things.

Perry gathered himself, thought for a while, brushed himself off, turned around to face his fallen chair, picked it up, turned around again, and finally sat down with a sigh.

"Quit staring at me." Perry stood up.

"Stop coming on to me, you know?"

Perry looked down, trying to feign an unimpressed surprise.

Moony heard the distant sound of a faraway coyote howling. "You're weirding me out." Moony didn't like the way Perry looked at him. "Get out of here." He raised his fist and approached Perry, whose beer-goggled eyes indicated he might receive Moony with open arms, violence or no. He stopped at a distance, leaning back with his arms rigid in front of his belly, trying to summon the energy he had reserved from high school football by slacking off on the field, as if sloth possessed the power to send little packets of energy to himself in the future. Moony's stance sent a mixed message. His intended message: *Don't touch me with your phallus. Let's sit down and converse as before.* The conveyed one: *Come and get it. Hug me if you dare.* Moony was hardwired to be charming, so his body language often clued unwanted advances.

Two or three coyotes joined the howling. Some yips and barks, too.

Moony realized he was taking slow steps backward in the sand, his bare feet sinking deeper with each retreat. The wet grains pushed up between his toes, cold and gritty. Perry wasn't getting any farther away. If anything, he loomed larger, his shadow stretching long in the sunset. "Is this what they taught you at that federal training facility in Booker? How to interrogate someone with one of those things?"

Perry's laugh came out with a sound like sticking a shovel in a pile of gravel. "I'm not making advances, Moony. I just . . . I want to show you what I'm working with."

"I think this means you're probably at least a little gay, my friend."

Perry would question his sexuality three times in his life. This was the second. The third would provide an answer he didn't expect.

Perry stepped closer to him, and Moony knew if he started to run, Perry would somehow catch up, taking big, slow steps toward him. Perry had the keys to the RV. Moony knew they were in his pocket, jingling . . . jingling against what? Moony wanted to escape. He wanted to escape from the experience ever dawning.

He wanted to feel like someone else. A few hours into a chi-orienting video game and he would feel perfect again.

He fumbled with his hands. How to smooth this over? Now was not a time for conversation.

Perry told Moony that "It's not a big deal" then said that he should "Come here."

Instead, Moony ran like a scared rabbit.

❖ ❖ ❖

Moony was chased:

- across the road
- past concerned campers
- across another road
- into a bakery (past a fresh batch of maple donuts he thought twice about stopping for)
- into the kitchen
- out the back door
- through a line to the bathroom
- over a retaining wall and eventually
- onto the beach.

He was drunk and fried from amphetamines, so he decided it would be prudent to head for the water and start swimming.

Perry stopped at the water's edge, dizzy. He vomited on a sandcastle.

Moony continued his excursion into the Sea of Cortez. He felt determined to disappear. He would not look back. He would savor drowning if that's what it took to maintain composure. When he got tired of the forward stroke, he began to backstroke. Unfortunately, he had the conditioning of an elite athlete, and what might have been twenty minutes of panicked swimming barely winded him. Treading water in the dark sea, he looked around to see that he'd lost sight of land entirely. The night clouds and stars overwhelmed him. What a terrible thing to witness, he felt, at first regarding Perry's all-embracing open-ended exuberance, later regarding the night sky. Three distinct impulses warred in him as he floated:

First, the trained response—or what he'd convinced himself was training: analyze Perry's vulnerability for leverage. The man's loneliness made him exploitable. Moony knew that Perry's emotions were kinked; he felt jealous, and somewhere there was a twinge of actual attraction, but mostly it was a sort of self-pitying envy that had got him going. So what was the game worth playing here?

Perry had connections Moony hadn't seriously considered. The man mentioned his federal training facility work, those visitors from Washington taking suspects away. Perry knew people. Not the flashy contractors everyone knew about, but the quiet ones. The infrastructure people. If the Gypsy's operation was what Moony suspected, then Perry's contacts could actually be valuable. A former cop with federal facility experience, now running a suburban bar? Decent cover and placement.

Which meant the second possibility: that Perry might already have been recruited. This whole scene could be operational—test Moony's responses, create compromising material, establish control. Classic honeypot, just sloppier than usual.

More likely, Perry was exactly what he seemed: a lonely divorced landlord with a hard-on and too many beers. Perry was just another nobody trying to connect with someone, anyone. Even if that connection came out sideways and drunk and embarrassing. If that was the case, it left Moony feeling envious of Perry's ability to want something so inarticulately. To reach for connection without any strategy or self-protection that might all be imaginary anyway.

The fact that he felt all three simultaneously made him wonder if he'd ever have a single authentic emotion in his life. Maybe this was what Yvette had tried to tell him–that their background didn't make them powerful. It made them hollow.

A thought came to him in a strange voice, like his own but older and with a speech impediment: *You ithh doing nothhhing wiff yauu life*. He could find proof of this in his address (few people dream of owning an address in an apartment complex called Sod Hill, his apartment number beginning with a Q) and in his soggy clothes (half the time he didn't even know what color shirt he had on, so why did he deserve any special attention from People Who Mattered?).

Waves of hatred toward his father that he'd never let himself acknowledge surged through him, colder than the water. He remembered one Christmas when he was twelve, opening the expensive watch from his father. Dan Senior had said, "Someday you'll be good enough to wear it." The casual cruelty of it. The way success was never enough, only the promise of future adequacy. Now he would finally be good enough–ruthless enough to earn the old man's approval by doing the very thing that would piss him off most. He'd say to hell with the family and start the endeavor with the Gypsy. She was horrid, but this would be his own thing. Perry had his barroom art screenings; Moony would launder money for oligarchs. He'd do it in earnest, too–no hedges, like a complete ass–not to gather intel or to play at a bigger game.

The thought of Yvette pierced him. She'd made the right move, the only move that preserved any dignity. If only he'd been there for her, if only he'd recognized what she was telling him. But no, he'd been angry at her for articulating what he felt, for being more in touch with the truth than he was. He understood now: to have anything in this world, you must do terrible things either to yourself or to others. Yvette had purchased the most high-priced upgrade of all–she'd bought her way out completely.

He cried, not deeply but enough to count as weeping. He knew that if anyone were watching, they would see something to the effect of a crying man. For a brief moment, he was not conscious of himself. He wept, not because he was chased down by a drunk landlord or because of the night sky, and he didn't need to know he was shivering in the fifty-degree water. The alcohol had thinned his blood. The beer had dehydrated his muscles.

He floated in peace for a while, his negative thoughts and ideas nursed away by the action of water. The tide carried him back to shore.

Perry sat in the sand watching the sea return his friend to him. A young couple, not twenty feet from him, undulated awkwardly enough to be real, making a love sandwich between a blanket and a beach towel. He listened to the breath and body sounds but did not look. Perry had no revelation.

Moony waded onto shore. If Perry made a move at this point, Moony would punch him in the face. He would kick his overeager crotch. Then later he would tell Deb everything.

"Sorry, buddy," said Perry, sand in his beard. He had his hand raised. It reminded Moony of Tom Hanks's character in the movie *Castaway*. He felt sad.

Moony didn't know what to say. The two men walked decently for a while, side by side.

Moony nearly had an even more substantial life revelation but was interrupted; Perry put his arm around him. At first, it was awkward. After a time, Moony realized he would be wrong to interpret the motion as anything but a brotherly gesture from a friend, and he put his arm around Perry's shoulder.

Perry stopped, and Moony turned to him, expecting to hear him elaborate on his apology. He prepared himself to greet the man with forgiveness and understanding. Now would be the time. Now would be the time for some sort of explanation.

Perry told him to quit making such a big deal out of it. Then he pulled it out. There it was, hanging more or less straight out of his zipper's opening. If someone were to have walked by, they would have seen two grown men standing facing each other, motionless for four seconds, looking down at the waist-level object.

"Are we gonna swordfight or what?" asked Perry, enjoying the hell out of himself again. "Come on, you've given it so much attention already."

"No way, Jose," said Moony, stepping back.

Perry wagged forward. Moony reached his hand into Perry's pocket; wrenched out the keys thinking, *This right here which I am doing, I am not doing, no hand in the pants;* and he bolted.

Hopping inside the RV, he started the engine then locked the doors.

Was he just going to leave his landlord in Mexico?

He could. Maybe twelve people in the world would care.

What kind of friend does that?

He didn't know.

What kind of friend chases his pal down the beach with a surprise erection? He could guess at the answer to that: a bastard named Perry Whitecomb.

He put the RV in gear and sped forward.

In fact, he kept driving. It felt good.

Things could continue this way—just him, the empty RV, the open road, and the distant memory of a strange woolly man far behind him.

After a couple of minutes, he swung the RV around and returned to the last known whereabouts of the man in white linen slacks.

Moony saw him illuminated in the headlights. He was pissing a long stream at a high angle of attack by the side of the road.

Moony unlocked the passenger door and let him in. He smelled like a bad night.

"Let's forget about this," Perry said.

Moony kept his eyes on the road. "Before we forget about it, let me ask you something."

Perry shifted in his seat, the leather creaking.

"That whole scene back there—was that you, or was that someone's idea?"

"What?" Perry's voice cracked.

"You know who my family is." Moony's hands tightened on the wheel. "So either you're working for someone and this was some amateur attempt at compromising material, or you're just a lonely drunk who got confused about what kind of trip this was."

Perry was quiet for a long moment. "They wanted me to keep an eye on the Adams kid who very suspiciously became a tenant at Sod Hill. 'Let us know if anything goes down.'"

"Who's 'they'?"

"It doesn't matter," Perry said.

Moony glanced over. Perry was staring out the side window at the darkness.

"Though if I'm being honest," Perry continued, "I figured either way I'd learn something about you. Either you'd fight me, or you'd run—which you did—or you'd play along."

"Except you puked on a sandcastle."

"Not my finest hour." Perry turned to look at him. "So what happens now? You gonna call your dad and get me fired?"

Moony thought about it. The way Perry said it made it sound so ordinary. Like someone, perhaps even Moony's own parents, had asked Perry to keep an eye on problem tenants, not conduct surveillance on a valuable asset. "I think we really do forget about it. The drunk part, anyway. But if you're taking someone's money to watch me, that needs to stop."

"Or what?"

"I know how these things work, Perry. What you risk isn't worth the extra income for looking the other way."

Perry scratched his nose. "Jesus, Moony. You make it sound like some spy movie. They just wanted to know if you were causing trouble or if anyone weird came around asking about you."

"So it was my parents."

"Jeez, man. You really think your own parents would pick a guy like me to keep an eye on you? Your dad's got government contracts, and Adams Minerals has fingers in a lot of pies. No, some folks get nervous when the boss's son goes off script. And they maybe think they see an opening for them."

The way Perry said it made Moony's theories seem credible. But that was exactly what someone would say if they were really good at their cover. Or if they were just a property manager who'd been asked to keep an eye on tenants. The problem with learning to see conspiracies everywhere was that you could never tell the difference between actual conspiracies and your own paranoia eating its own tail.

"Here's what I think," Moony continued. "Whoever it is, you take their money, but you hate yourself for it. That's why you do these movie screenings, trying to build something real. That's why you got drunk and chased me down the beach—not because you wanted to bone, but because you hoped I would do something to blow up the whole arrangement."

"Jesus Christ," Perry said.

"So here's the deal. You stop reporting on me, and I don't burn your operation. Because unlike you, Perry, I actually know how to disappear people."

Even as he said it, Moony wondered what the hell "disappearing people" would actually involve. He'd never disappeared anyone. He'd helped Kitty clean an apartment that may or may not have contained evidence of an actual crime. But Perry didn't need to know the extent of his inexperience.

"Horseshit."

But then Perry went quiet, which meant either Moony had hit something true or Perry was too tired to keep arguing with a rich kid's spy fantasies. The silence stretched long enough that Moony started to wonder if he'd overplayed his hand.

The RV hummed. Finally Perry spoke.

"They'll know something's changed if I stop sending reports."

Despite the fact that Perry's statement indicated that he was indeed a target of actual espionage, relief flooded through Moony. He'd been right. Or at least partially right. Or Perry was humoring him. It was impossible to tell the difference anymore.

"Then send them boring ones. I play video games. I fuck my girlfriend and my landlord. Nothing worth noting."

"And if they send someone else?"

Moony smiled—he hoped without humor. It brought an end to the conversation.

He drove back to the beach, and the two men hit the hay, separately in the sand. Before nodding off, Perry reminisced about when he was nineteen in Utah on a road trip, when experimentation had a more fruitful outcome. The "Have you ever?" game ended in fun that once; he had never again managed to convince the world that very few things in life were big deals. These days, every interaction came with paperwork in his mind–who'd want to know about it, what it might mean, whether it was worth reporting.

❖ ❖ ❖

On the return drive, the twelve-cylinder engine brought the RV screaming down the flat, wondrous Arizona highway.

"How's the temperature? You good?" asked Perry.

He still had sand in his beard, and he wore new sunglasses from the gas station in Why, Arizona. These were aviator-style frames, which suited him well.

Moony watched as Perry polished off the last of the continental breakfast hot dogs they'd picked up at a gas station. It was a folded waffle stuffed with a hot dog, instant oatmeal, and grape jelly.

"Oh yeah. Temperature's good."

Moony had not forgotten the events of last night. He was sure that he was acting as if he had. In his mind, he kept flashing back to the chase, reinventing key details and making everything worse. The situation became more vivid than he could have perceived in his condition. It became more cartoonish and Jungian—in his memory, Perry had the head of a jackal and was carrying a glass jar containing Yvette's last breath. In the man's pocket were his father's severed hands on a silver keychain, signing document after document.

Moony had just awoken from a fatigued state of dehydration brought about by the beer. He drank just one beer shy of a baker's dozen because he didn't know when to stop and because Perry had convinced him there would be no harm in overdoing it. Today, he was not so sure.

While Perry seemed to understand how to go about his morning hung over and accepted the state as a necessary evil, Moony could not. He got up and walked to the rear of the RV, pondering the cases of Mexican beer.

"Is it illegal to drink in a moving vehicle if you're sitting way back here?"

"Mmm."

"Will it help the hangover?"

"No. But it always helps me."

Moony cracked open a beer. Sweet Jesus, that was going to do the trick. He knew it. He could hear the sweet relief.

"You want to bring me one?" asked Perry with a grin, exaggerating his overbite. "Highway patrol on this interstate are pretty lax, should be fine," he said to himself.

Moony watched as the cars zoomed by, remembering the night. He wondered how a different man would have handled the situation. "You know I actually really like Deb, don't you?" Moony regretted speaking.

Perry choked back something. "Here. You take the wheel. I'm gonna piss."

After retching up two or three continental breakfast hot dogs into their coffee can, Perry's voice echoed from the RV's bathroom. "I don't blame her," he said. "She's solid and grounded and full of love. Christ, I don't blame you, either. It's just nature. It doesn't change anything just when a person knows something. What she and I have is good. I've been happy. Why should I complain just because I know about it now? If it'd been a problem, it would've been so whether you told me or not."

Moony stared at the highway ahead.

Perry's partial confession from last night clicked into place.

Moony wasn't the asset awaiting activation. He was the bait.

Sure, it was his choice to park in some nowhere suburb, but that didn't stop people from trying to use him anyway. He was like a bug light for international interests. They wanted to see who showed up. Of course his family was keeping tabs on him. But someone else was, too. Look who had already showed up: first it was Russians looking to launder money, next it might be Chinese interested in lithium connections, cartels wanting new routes. In the bar that night, he'd made the mistake of using a pickup line with Kitty alluding to the possibility that he was some sort of spy, and she'd connected him with her sister, who actually knew how to use such people.

And Perry—Perry had actually confessed that he was at least one of the guys who was reporting on him for someone.

Sure, maybe Perry was just a property manager who'd been asked to keep an eye on a rich kid, and Moony's mind was turning routine surveillance into something out of a John le Carré novel. But even if that was true, the principle remained the same: Moony knew his family wouldn't miss the opportunity to take advantage of his position while letting him believe he was rebelling. Which meant the Gypsy might not be recruiting him in earnest. She could be checking if he was still bait or if he'd been activated. Testing whether the family had finally brought him in or if he was still sitting there, drawing interest while thinking he was choosing his own path.

Every gesture of independence—nothing could stop him from becoming part of someone else's operation. Even doing nothing could be somebody's strategy. Or maybe he was giving his family too much credit, and the Gypsy was just a money launderer who'd heard about a bored rich kid. She had basically told him something to this effect in his apartment. She'd come over to test him, and he'd failed, but she still wanted to use him.

"Listen," Moony said, keeping his eyes on the road. "If people are paying attention to me, they're probably paying attention to everyone at Sod Hill. You really need to be careful what you put in writing. Like I said last night. Keep it boring. Video games and beer, nothing worth noting."

Perry was quiet for a long moment. "That's the plan. You good up there?" he called from the bathroom.

By way of response, the RV hit a pothole and sloshed the coffee can.

"Yeah," Moony lied. "I'm good."

❖ ❖ ❖

Heath stood at Moony's stovetop, the spatula trembling in his hand like a divining rod. One side of the scrambled eggs had burned while he'd been watching them transform from uncooked to cooked, but he didn't mind.

The spatula began to hum.

Heath brought it closer to his face to study the cheap plastic handle.

"You're going to lose your job," the spatula informed him. "Thursday. The chief will say it's about response times, but really it's because you told Martinez that the station's dog was planning something."

Heath set the spatula down carefully on the counter. It was mathematically impossible for a spatula to be wrong about employment matters.

He returned his gaze to the eggs. "Knowing the future isn't something you have to feel only one way about," he told them. He nodded, scraped the eggs onto a plate, and placed the spatula gently in the sink.

❖ ❖ ❖

Moony got home to find his front door unlocked and the place smelling of burned eggs, but the money and everything else in his apartment was undisturbed. In the front room, anyway. He walked into the bedroom and saw his shelves of vintage video games all intact, too.

Ninja Gaiden caught his eye. Twenty minutes of that would settle his nerves. The way you had to memorize exactly where each bird would spawn and dive, how the game punished you for moving too fast or too slow. The game didn't want you to win. It wanted you to earn progress through repetition and pain. Some nights he'd play the same section fifty times, dying to the same enemy, until his thumbs went numb and his eyes burned, and suddenly he'd nail the pattern perfectly and sail through untouched.

No. He didn't need good chi for what he was about to do.

If he started playing now, he'd never leave.

He grabbed his car keys and put the Gypsy's money into a duffel bag.

It was now or never.

❖ ❖ ❖

Moony shook hands with a short, oily man in the office of Aurora AAAA Storage, a man named Carl, as Carl explained why this particular facility was "primo rill state." The facility was surrounded by a double layer of eight-foot chain-link fence with razor wire sandwiched between, protecting a maze of nondescript sheet metal buildings with rusted roll-up doors in Aurora's industrial district. Carl had the demeanor of someone for whom big dreams were a comical impossibility.

The Gypsy's money sat in a duffel bag over Moony's shoulder.

"Now, I know what you're thinking," Carl said. "I always know exactly what people are thinking. It's why I'm in sales. You're thinking storage units aren't sexy. But they're steady income. People put their stuff in, months and years go by, and there's nothing we have to do, yet they keep paying. There's no better investment on God's green Earth. To me, that's sexy."

They were standing outside now. Carl droned on about how the facility was impervious to fires and any act of God save perhaps an earthquake. He seemed terrified by the mere thought of them. Moony was currently in buyer mode; he didn't bother reassuring Carl that the threat of earthquakes capable of damaging storage units was nonexistent in Colorado.

At Moony's stoic nod, Carl felt obliged to confess that one whole wing of the complex had occasionally suffered from "water infiltration from overhead" but hastened to add there was absolutely no trace of moisture damage anymore and definitely no pests—he'd seen to that personally.

"The roofs leak," Moony translated aloud.

Carl winced.

"How many units are occupied?" Moony asked.

"About sixty percent occupied right now, but that's because the previous owner let things slide. New management could get that up to ninety percent easy." Carl leaned forward conspiratorially. "And here's the beautiful part—when people stop paying, after proper notice, of course, you get to auction off their stuff. Last month we cracked open a unit—guy was six months behind. Found a whole vintage guitar collection. Auction brought in eight grand, pure profit. Best decision I ever made."

"What if they come back for their things?"

"That's the beauty of the contract," Carl said, tapping his forehead, as if that's where the contracts were housed. "After ninety days of nonpayment, it's yours. You'd be surprised what people abandon. Photo albums, family heirlooms, sometimes even cars. It's like ..." He searched for words. "Like being an archaeologist."

Moony watched as a woman in oversize gray sweats and a Yankees cap loaded a box of ceiling fans into a unit.

"I had one unit," Carl continued, warming to his theme. "Lady stored her whole life in there after a divorce. Beautiful, beautiful woman." He made the universal sign language for "curvy woman" with his hands. "Paid for two years, then nothing. When we opened it up—wedding dress still in plastic, kids' toys, even her old yearbooks. Sold it all for pennies on the dollar to dealers.

That's the business—we're storing the stuff people can't let go of. Until they do."

"Sounds predatory," Moony said.

"It's a service," Carl corrected. "We give them time to get their lives together. Not our fault if they don't."

"I'll take it," Moony said.

Carl blinked. "Of course, you'll want to see the books. Tour the facilities a bit more. I've got three years of—"

"Cash deal. We can close this week."

"There are inspections, paperwork—"

Moony opened the duffel bag just enough for Carl to see the neat stacks inside. "Two hundred thousand now. The rest I'm sure you'll be happy to carry a note on. That way we can expedite things."

Carl's expression shifted from fear to hunger to rapture. A bead of sweat dropped from his eyebrow onto his lower lip.

"You're one hell of a salesman, Carl. I look at you, and I see the man I hope to become. I'm a romantic. And this is a business I know I'll fall in love with. I can't think of a better way of investing my inheritance," Moony said, which, for a load of malarkey, was true enough. Everything was inheritance if you traced it back far enough, you see.

Within an hour, they'd drawn up preliminary papers. Moony signed them with his left hand, making his signature portray the kind of intellect of one who would leap into such a situation. The LLC he'd formed online—Managed Investment & Lease Facilities (MILF)—would own the property.

As he left, Carl called after him. "There's just one thing I should let you know. Most storage facilities have a few units that are off limits. Previous owner had some arrangement. Units 147 through 153. They pay triple rate, always on time, no questions asked."

"Of course," Moony said.

Driving back to Denver, Moony felt nothing in particular about becoming a property owner. He'd just converted the Gypsy's investment into something concrete, boring, and useful.

At a red light, he noticed the woman in the Yankees cap in the car beside him. She was crying.

Now he owned a piece of that economy.

❖ ❖ ❖

Perry locked the door inside Frog House and turned to face the empty bar. Thirty chairs arranged in a wide crescent moon. He'd tested each one for wobbles, tightening loose screws with the Leatherman his father had given him, back when Perry still thought he'd take over the bee business.

"Welcome, everyone, to tonight's screening," he said to the empty room, then shook his head. He unscrewed the bottle of Gatorade and took a swig.

He tried again, looser, with a smile. "Hey folks, glad you could make it out on this beautiful morning."

The chairs stared back.

He walked to chair fifteen, where that quiet girl Yvonne would sit tomorrow if she came, and adjusted it a bit to the left to give it a better line of sight to the screen.

"You know, when I first started these screenings," he began, practicing his pre-movie talk, "I thought—"

He stopped. In the reflection against the glass of the bar's back wall, he noticed that his fly was down.

"Goddammit."

It was completely open. Had been all day. Through the meeting with the beer distributor. Through his conversation with the woman about Italian neorealism. Through everything.

"I thought film could change lives," he told the empty room, zipping up.

Out of habit when caught in a compromising situation, Perry turned to look behind him. Two jackets lay on the back bench, arranged so one sleeve fell across the other. Outerwear spooning like sleeping lovers. He smiled and turned to face the chairs again.

"Did you all realize that the man who sold me this bar died three weeks later? Heart attack in a Wendy's drive-through. His wife sent me his notebooks. Forty years of writing down what the weather was like, what he ate that day, and the names of new people he met. Every single day. I have them in the basement. Forty years of that. Can you imagine?"

He looked to see what the chairs thought about that.

❖ ❖ ❖

After returning home from Aurora AAAA Storage, Moony checked his email to find his family had sent him a message. Instead of deleting it, he decided he would read what they sent. It seemed they were sending him on some kind of mission. He was beside himself with excitement but reread it to make sure.

He checked the *from* field. It wasn't a familiar address, but the domain certainly belonged to his family: kellner_holdings@adamsmineral.com. The subject line read:

Fwd.: fw: fw: collection

The email chain was frustratingly brief:

>>>*just send adams to JJ*

>>*which adams?*

>*whichever one is around. he'll open for that name*

>>>>>>> *A112 has what you need*

>>>>>> *Who's the contact?*

That was all there was to the message.

Moony's return journey from Mexico had taken longer and been less boisterous than the trip to Mexico, and it had been unassisted by any stimulants besides those manufactured by his body in times of need. And he'd done no chi-centering since returning. Yet he was surprised how reading this message from his family gave him a spike of hope in this otherwise radio-silent chapter of life. It was a silence he'd fought for but now wished he hadn't. He hated to think of himself living some prairie wife existence of no consequence, as if waiting for a message that may never come. He was raised to feel valuable. Valuableness was a feeling he could disappear into. Yvette didn't understand.

Moony sorted through what he believed to be the intended facts.

Starting from the fact that it was sent to him, he could take for certain that he was the Adams being referred to, which meant they believed this was all the information needed to unravel the message.

JJ, then, could refer to Jon-Jon, the storyteller clown he'd met a few days prior at the *King Kong* screening, the one who'd made Perry cry with the giraffe story. To be sure, it was beyond implausible that his family could take any interest in Jon-Jon, who, from all appearances, scored so high on the loser chart as to be in the realm of absolute inconceivability. Moony found the belief systems of all normal people something to look down on, but he found it impossible to believe that even in a world of billions, there could be an individual like Jon-Jon whose ambition was to be a clown. There had to be more to him. The drug world had plenty of guys you could rely on to do odd jobs. What could Jon-Jon possibly have that his family could find of use? The kicker was that he was pretty sure Jon-Jon lived in apartment A112.

As always, it would be nice if coded messages were a little more forthcoming. Maybe the compliance officer had redacted sensitive information. From appearances, it was a conversation between two other people and was sent to him by someone he didn't know personally for no clear reason—or perhaps the reason was exactly what it appeared to be: they needed an Adams, any Adams, and he was the one who happened to be around.

Deliberation, he decided, would do no good. These people were zeroes. He'd risk nothing by just poking around to see what turned up.

After the successful purchase of Aurora AAAA Self Storage by MILF and the gift of this new purpose, Moony had an abundance of energy, so he walked all the way across the parking lot with Celia to Jon-Jon's house. Makeup concealing her black eye, she watched the snow fall.

Moony knocked on number 112's door, just like the message had wanted him to.

So far, so good.

No one answered.

Moony knocked again, harder. He rang the doorbell.

The door opened. A man about Moony's age, with thick glasses and urban caveman hair, stood and regarded Moony with disgust.

"Jon-Jon home?" said Moony.

"Who the *freak* wants to know?"

Moony figured he'd found his man, even though this man wasn't Jon-Jon. He called into the room behind the door's caveman guardian: "Jon-Jon? You have a minute?"

The apartment was a role-playing-game fanatic's dream. The walls were lined with gray steel shelving units where dragon figurines fought hordes of trolls beneath vast quantities of house dust. Posters of elf girls in chain mail dominated all available walls and ceiling.

The near-sighted Cro-Magnon grinned at Celia for a moment and let them in.

"Jon-Jon's holding out, and I'm here to collect," said Moony, like the detective he fantasized about hiring.

"We paid Heath yesterday," he said. "What, you need a receipt?"

Moony looked around the apartment, wondering if a receipt would cut it. The place looked like a ferret cage.

The caveman ambled over to a water cooler, beside which was a mason jar of water, drank long mouthfuls from it, and stood there breathing hard like a child might. The effect of this on Moony was that he realized how goddamn thirsty he was. He realized he hadn't drunk anything besides beer for the past two days.

"Go ahead, give Heath a call."

Moony was about to confess that he didn't have his phone on him, but he stayed detective instead. He was confident he was bringing the pieces together.

"Oh yeah? What's all this about Heath? I said I'm here to collect."

The caveman looked at Celia, who wore a cute green sweater and gray skirt. Celia shot him a glance that said clearly *Please don't.*

The caveman rotated his head to fix his gaze back on Moony. "You want some water? Those jars are fresh. The cooler's been funky lately." He filled a glass from a mason jar. "We get it from this woman who does alkaline treatments. Says it opens your perception channels. Probably bullshit, but it tastes all right."

Moony, seated on a couch littered with shredded newspaper, drank the glass of water the man brought him in a style much like the caveman. Afterward, he didn't like how it tasted somewhat bitter and metallic and smelled like peaches. He dismissed the doubt as soon as it surfaced.

"Takes about twenty minutes to feel different," the caveman said, then caught himself. "I mean, if you believe in that stuff."

"So what kind of racket are you up to here?" Moony asked.

The caveman nodded slowly and was surprisingly forthcoming, glad someone was taking an interest. "Mostly crypto. We're in the sending-and-receiving business. There's plenty of stuff out there that you can hack, and if you use a North Korean endpoint, people assume the obvious and leave you the hell alone. That, and a side gig running game servers. Ain't that hard here to bypass the power meter and get free juice."

Moony had a sinking feeling in his chest. Some people had "soon to be incarcerated" written on them. No way in hell was this what the message had meant. Or if it was what the message had meant, it meant he was an ass. He'd just stormed into a stranger's apartment and asked stupid questions.

Was that the point? The thought crept in. *Did someone send this just to make sure I knew how left out I was?*

Outside the window, he could hear laughter from somewhere in the parking lot. Even strangers were having a better time than he was.

A noise rumbled from the bathroom, and out came a man wearing black.

"Meet Ricardo."

"Moony. Pleased to meet you. I have heard many good things about you," said Ricardo. "I will be performing soon at a new theater, the Spirit World. I do magic."

"I'm not much of a performer myself," said Moony.

Ricardo lit a cigarillo by snapping his fingers. He offered Moony one.

"No, thanks."

"One for the lady?"

"No, thanks."

"Suit yourself."

"We should be getting off now," said Moony, beginning to feel strange in the presence of a caped man.

The caveman bid farewell. "I pity you, Moony the man. I'll call the Gypsy and tell her you came by and did just what she told you to."

"What'd you say?" Moony asked, his voice sharper than intended.

The caveman was one of those people who could adjust their glasses by making a sort of sneery face and squinting. "She said you'd come by eventually. And that it's not good to ignore someone who's been generous with you. Said you'd be asking questions about Jon-Jon. But he moved out, man. It's crazy what that woman knows."

Of course. Of fucking course.

The email wasn't from his family at all—she'd somehow spoofed their domain or something. And he'd walked right into it like an amateur. He'd been so hungry for proof that he mattered, that he was part of something important, that he'd practically gift wrapped himself for whatever game she was actually playing. She would probably be pissed at him for just going ahead and buying the storage place without consulting whoever her keeper of the threshold was.

The caveman was still talking and occasionally gesturing at some of the posters, but Moony couldn't focus on the words. He'd underestimated the Gypsy as just a small-time grifter who'd correctly guessed that a bored rich kid would jump at the chance to feel like an asset, but it was possible she was some sort of master manipulator who'd been watching him for months.

Both possibilities made him feel like an idiot, but for completely different reasons.

Was this her way of proving a point? That she could make him dance whenever she wanted? Or was this just what happened when you spent your whole life waiting for someone to activate you—eventually, any activation would do?

The bitter water sat heavy in his stomach. He glanced at Celia, who smiled at him and gave him a look that said she was ready to leave now.

"When did Jon-Jon move out?" he asked, trying to keep his voice casual.

"Jon-Jon split, like, two weeks ago, something about the D and D group falling apart," the caveman said.

Moony nodded dully and turned to leave.

"Oh, wait," the caveman called. "She said to give you this if you showed up."

He tossed Moony a small key. It looked like a safety deposit box key. But no—it was probably for one of the storage units.

"She say what it's for?"

The caveman shrugged. "Said you'd know what it went to."

Moony didn't want to give himself away. He pocketed the key, opened the door, and left.

◆ ◆ ◆

Moony decided not to give the event a second thought for a while.

He and Celia went to King Soopers to pick up some groceries. The two had planned on making frozen pizzas tonight. Celia had been watching a lot of cooking shows.

"We should get some more houseplants, honey," Celia said, puffy eyed.

"Another ivy?"

"A cactus." She smiled at him sweetly. "Let's get a few of them."

They kissed. An onlooker looked on, possibly jealous, maybe judgmental. People do that kind of thing.

King Soopers's color scheme was yellow and bright red. The store smelled like fish and fruit. Celia picked out miniature cacti while Moony browsed the Italian section. He was fairly sure they were in love. He felt a little sick, then, a few aisles later, much sicker, more exhausted. The world was such a rotten apricot to him. His eyes were no longer concerned with negotiating solid shapes; he began seeing a swimming yellow and vivid red and dropped to the floor, convulsing. His body struggled with contradictory impulses to curl into fetal position and break apart, skull first. He vomited and passed out.

When Celia came around the corner, cactus in one hand, the other hand rubbing a peach's fuzz on her lower lip, she had no clue what to do except to hug him and call for help. His eyes were wide open, helpless; she saw all the constellations in them.

Moony, meanwhile, wasn't in communication with the surface world at all. He could hear the song playing inside Celia's head—it was a song by George Harrison called *Ding Dong*, and it sounded like it was being played on vinyl. He was really out of it, so he took each new unconscious moment to be more real than the previous one under the energy-saving bulbs of the grocery store. Where he was now, a medium-size auburn dog of mixed breed stood in a black plastic room.

Moony was the first to speak. "Who's a good boy? Come here— who's a good boy?" He extended his hand, but there was nothing in it but affection.

He held it there, lightheaded.

After a minute, he came back to the world. He had no idea what to remember. It seemed that only a moment ago, the auburn dog was headed toward his hand, which was a nice gesture of companionship between animals. And now a woman was near him. The dog was certainly a male. He learned from the female that he cared for a familiar-looking girl named Celia, and then he even remembered his name was Moony.

The rest of the day's events had escaped him. He learned he could trust her.

When he stood up, he looked down and discovered he had wet his pants. That was a first.

Leaving the cactus and peach in the aisle, she led him to her car, and he got inside, feeling nothing if not a vague gratitude for life. He had been repressing his enjoyment of love.

* * *

A semi-shiny green 1978 Chevrolet Caprice Classic sped into the left lane next to Celia's Celica.

It was Perry, happy as hell to see the couple on the road. He listened to the R&B station on the radio. The volume was at a decent level for the deaf.

Excited honking ensued.

"Pull over! Pull over! Hey, buddy! Celia!"

The horn stuck down, and the honking continued in a resounding, solid twelve-volt Chevrolet note.

"Shit!" Randomly frantic, he turned down the volume on the radio. "Shit. Uh . . ."

He realized that he could pull the fuse for the horn. Then he realized he was driving his car forty-seven miles per hour down the road, then he noticed that the road was Broadway Avenue. Then he found that he had strayed onto the median. His final decision was to wait until he pulled over to get into the fuse box.

Celia slowed down and followed his Chevrolet when he turned into the Home Depot parking lot, horn blaring. Moony, head bumping against the car window at every turn, moaned an obsolete jingle for Rug Doctor carpet shampooers.

"Sorry about that," Perry explained, exiting his car energetically, carrying his fourth Red Bull of the day.

Celia was visibly put out. "Just fix it," she said.

He reached below the dash and pulled out a fuse, a second fuse, another fuse, a fourth and fifth fuse, and the horn stopped.

"Well, my brake lights don't work now, so do me a favor and follow me to Sod Hill? I don't want to get rear-ended." Perry gawked at Moony. "You guys party hearty or something?"

"Uh, he got sick." Celia took this personally.

Smacking on Chiclets, Perry looked into the car at Moony, who gazed back behind heavy eyelids. A cattle truck passed by, leaving the stench of cow shit.

"Moony." Perry knocked on the glass. "Moony, I need a favor. Let me borrow your car tomorrow. I need it to impress a lady. Mine, the passenger seat—occasionally there's a glue residue when it's hot, sticks to your pants." His words left a fog on the window that wouldn't wipe away.

Moony nodded.

"She's a hot one."

"Hot."

"We should double date."

"Date." Moony laid his head back and closed his eyes.

Celia said, "He's not himself. You got a date? What about Deb?"

Perry finished his Red Bull and tossed it onto the pavement. It chuffed into a small drift of snow.

"Yeah, well, only live once."

❖ ❖ ❖

Exiting Home Depot, Heath spotted Celia and said, "What would Jesus do?"

Deciding it was to throw stones at the car, he searched for a rock that spoke to him. Patiently listening for a half hour, the group was gone by the time he found one, so he put the rock in his pocket.

"I am your friend," said the rock. Heath had never been happier.

❖ ❖ ❖

"Technical support, this is Josh; can I get your account number?"

The call center occupied what used to be a shopping mall—three football fields of cubicles under forty-foot ceilings where the skylights had been painted black. During the day shift, sunlight leaked through the paint in spiderweb patterns.

Josh had to present an ID badge, scan his palm, and pass two different checkpoints to reach his cubicle. The first scanner was at the main entrance, built into what used to be the perfume counter. The second was where the escalators had been ripped out, leaving a rectangular wound in the floor they'd surrounded with infographical banners. The third scanner was at the entrance to his section—what the auditor team called "The Cathedral" because of how voices echoed up into the vaulted ceiling.

His cubicle sat in what used to be Men's Activewear. The carpet still showed the ghost outlines of the old display islands. Sometimes he imagined mannequins in golf shirts watching him work.

"I'm showing a signal loss on your receiver. Let's start with a simple reset. Can you locate your receiver's power button?"

While the customer fumbled around and breathed heavily into the phone, Josh drew an inverted pentacle on his notepad. Above him, the industrial air system droned. Hundreds of cubicles inhaling customer complaints, exhaling scripted solutions. He was certain this was a truly powerful domain—all these voices channeled through headsets, all this suffering processed and cataloged. If any place could open a portal to the actual underworld, it would be here.

"Perfect. Now press and hold the power button for thirty seconds. This will initiate what we call a hard reset."

The customer started telling him about their grandson. Josh wrote LONELINESS IS THE ONLY TRUE GOD in his margin, then responded, "That sounds wonderful, ma'am. Your receiver should be booting up. What do you see on your screen now?"

She said she saw nothing. This irritated Josh, as it should have. "What does this nothing look like to you? Is it black, blue, static?" Josh pressed the mute button. "Or did you shut your goddamned TV off?" Then: "Let's check your connections. The cable from your wall should connect to the port labeled Satellite In."

Twenty minutes later, her TV worked. She was crying with gratitude. She said that calling Josh was the best decision she'd ever made.

"Is there anything else I can help you with today?"

There wasn't.

"Well, then, have a blessed day."

He meant it differently than she thought. Or maybe not.

❖ ❖ ❖

Moony sat in his apartment, staring at the Gypsy's key. On it was a piece of tape with the number 150 written on it.

Something wasn't adding up. If his family was using his position at Sod Hill as bait, someone should be monitoring who approached him. Yet nobody had warned him about the omnipresent theater owner or the goddamn poisoned caveman water.

But maybe he wasn't bait—maybe he was just a disappointment they'd encouraged being parked in suburbia because it would keep him out of trouble. And he'd gone beyond his depth.

The secure phone his father had given him sat in the drawer like a prop from a movie he wasn't actually starring in. After pacing for twenty minutes, he made a decision. He picked up the phone and dialed his brother Alex. If there was a breach, Alex would know. If there was anything to know.

The line rang four times before connecting.

"I need to know if we have a compromise situation."

Alex didn't miss a beat. "Location?"

"Denver. Suburban cover."

"Contact description?"

"Female. Eastern European. Possibly Romanian. Connected to theater operations."

"Known affiliations?"

"Still assessing. She may have infrastructure—I found evidence of a document fabrication network."

"Hold on one second." A click, then Alex's voice sounded farther off. Room sounds. "How did she approach?"

"Through an intermediary. Then direct contact at my residence."

"Did she make an offer?"

"Quarter million. Ostensibly for property investment. I believe it's a recruitment overture."

"And you're maintaining plausible deniability?"

"Affirmative."

"What about the Finnish corridor? Any reference to Helsinki?"

"No, nothing like that."

"Interesting. And the money—was it sequential bills?"

"I didn't check."

"You didn't check." Alex's voice was grave. "That's the first thing you check."

"I know. I know. I'll verify."

"What color was the bag?"

"What?"

"The bag. The money bag. What color?"

"It was . . . a wooden box."

"Wooden. Jesus." Alex exhaled sharply. "Moony, listen to me carefully."

In the background, someone laughed.

"Hold on," Alex said, his voice moving away from the phone. "No, he's still going. Hold on." More laughter, a woman's voice.

"Alex. This is important."

"Sorry," He was back. "Where were we? Right. The wooden box. Yes, very significant. That's old school. That means she's connected to the, uh . . ."

"Who's there with you?"

"Hmm?"

"Who's laughing?"

Silence.

"Alex."

"It's just Morgan. From the office. We're prepping the Peruvian deck."

"You have me on speaker."

"No."

"You have me on speaker, and you're messing with me."

"No, no. Nothing like that." A pause. "Let's continue. One more question."

"Go ahead."

"What's her name? The contact."

"She calls herself the Gypsy."

Alex started laughing.

"'The Gypsy,'" he repeated. "Oh my god. The Gypsy. That's—" He was wheezing now. "Hold on. Hold on. I have to—" The phone clattered. Distant laughter. Then he was back, catching his breath. "Sorry. Sorry. I just—'She calls herself the Gypsy.' Moony."

Moony thought again about the Gypsy's offer. Not for country or family, but for self. "Tell me what you know. What about Ecuador?" he asked.

Another pause, longer this time. "What do you know about Ecuador?"

"Just that it's been talked about."

"Not on any goddamn phone, it hasn't. And it sounds like you have problems of your own."

"I'm handling it."

"Handling it by taking a shot in the dark with me?" There was something in Alex's voice—genuine confusion. Like Ecuador meant lithium extraction and quarterly reports, not covert operations and geopolitical chess.

Moony closed his eyes. "By letting them think they've got me."

The silence stretched until Alex finally spoke. "Don't get creative, Moony. Just come in. We'll debrief you properly."

Debrief. The word felt both thrilling and hollow. What if there was nothing to debrief? What if "coming in" just meant joining the family mining business like any other nepotism hire?

"Never happening."

"This isn't a request."

"You're right about that much."

"You know what? Before you go, I should tell you—there was a note. Did you know that? Three pages. You were most of it."

"That's classified."

"It's not classified. It's a suicide note. She wrote about you. About how she couldn't—"

"Not on an open line."

"Moony."

"This conversation is over."

"She said she couldn't connect with you anymore. That you'd gone somewhere she couldn't reach."

Moony hung up before Alex could say more. He stared at the secure phone for a long moment, then went to the kitchen, found a hammer, and methodically destroyed it.

It was what a professional would do.

❖ ❖ ❖

Perry pulled up in the Sod Hill maintenance van, which he'd recently improved by adding magnetic signs reading WEEKEND WARRIOR MOBILE TOOL LIBRARY and NEED A TOOL? USE ME! The van's interior was packed full of power tools, wrench sets, lawnmowers, hardware, and useful gear of all kinds, complete with pegboard walls displaying everything from socket wrenches to tile saws.

"Check it out," Perry said as Moony climbed in. "People need tools for one project, right? But they don't want to buy a whole circular saw just to fix their deck. So I bring the tools to them. Like a bookmobile, but louder."

Moony nodded. He was noting that his friend had shaved off his beard but had kept a small devilish goatee. It was actually an improvement.

"The way I see it, I'm helping people help themselves. Think about it—how many times have you wanted to tackle a project but weren't able to because you didn't have all the right equipment?"

"That particular experience is not familiar to me," Moony said, unconsciously affecting the cadence of Data, the Starfleet android from *Star Trek*.

Perry nodded.

All the junk in the van knocked and rattled around so much it was impossible for Moony to hear Perry well enough to contribute to any sort of conversation outside the odd minute or two when Perry brought the unit to a full stop at an intersection. Perry discussed the kind of money a tool rental van could bring in. As he drove, he pointed out what he believed to be perfect DIY projects just waiting to happen and how he would advertise to potential clients the value of renting rather than owning.

"The real money is in recurring subscriptions. I've already got seven subscribers. I figure once I hit fifty, I can hire someone part time."

They drove east on Colfax, Perry explaining his plans for scheduled routes through neighborhoods, an app for reservations, maybe even on-premises classes on basic home repair.

They arrived at Aurora AAAA Self Storage. Moony's heart sank. He didn't introspect as to why this might be the case. Perry pulled the van into the spot nearest the dumpster. "That's a great parking job," he said. "Backing in there will make it easy to get out. Best decision I ever made."

Moony got out and unlocked the series of gates and doors necessary to set foot inside his new enterprise.

"You gotta love a good storage facility," Perry said with a grin. "It's like a mystery warehouse."

"That's the business model," Moony said.

"It's a central part of American society. How else could people preserve their memories when they own so much stuff?"

"I'm basically the Smithsonian."

Perry whacked Moony's arm. "Somebody's grumpy today."

Moony turned the Gypsy's key over in his fingers. "If I find any treasure, I'll give you twenty percent for driving me over."

They found unit 150 in the back corner of the complex. A woman in her sixties emerged from unit 146, dragging a mannequin dressed in a sequined gown.

"Oh!" She startled, dropping the mannequin. "Aren't you two handsome?"

Perry pointed to Moony. "Not only that, but you're talking to the new owner of the place."

"Wonderful! I'm Dotty. I'm hoping to start the county disco museum." She adjusted the mannequin's wig. "This is Stephanie. She's from my Studio 54 collection."

She was one of those women who had come to her later years altogether without any sort of grace, as if age had been an adversary who had simply called her up early one morning to deliver, suddenly, the worst news of personal catastrophe anyone had ever imagined. Her face was marked with the kind of lines that suggested she had been struck by emotions rather than come to them organically. She wore a purple tracksuit that had seen at least three better decades, but her hair, dyed a defiant shade of copper, was arranged in springy waves that carried sex appeal in any generation.

Perry's eyes lit up. "You have a disco museum?"

"If the county will fund my grant, I'll have the world's finest disco museum. I've gotten interest from senior centers, corporate events, tons of bar mitzvahs. People are out there, and they're dying to keep the dream alive." She looked at Moony hopefully. "The previous owner gave me a discount for cultural preservation. I don't suppose . . ."

"It all depends," Moony said stoically. "Some things are outside my hands. But let me ask you something. Giorgio Moroder or Nile Rodgers?"

Her face lit up like someone had just asked her to explain the meaning of life, and she actually knew the answer. "Oh honey, that's like asking someone to choose between breathing in and breathing out. Giorgio gave us the pulse. That synthetic heartbeat made you feel like you were living in the future. But Nile?" She clutched her chest. "Nile gave us soul. *The* soul. You can't have 'I Feel Love' without Giorgio, but you can't feel love without Nile."

Perry dropped a wad of chewing gum from his wide-open mouth. "Who's Giorgio—?"

"'Le Freak' or 'Good Times'?" Moony interrupted.

"'Good Times' for the bassline, 'Le Freak' for the breakdown. But if you really want to know Nile, you listen to what he did with Sister Sledge. 'Thinking of You' at two a.m. when the floor is still packed, but everyone's starting to couple up—that's church, young man."

"I'll talk it over with the board. We'll work something out," Moony said.

"Bless you. Oh, and word of advice. I saw someone go into 148 once at three in the morning dressed as a nun. But, like, a sexy nun? Very confusing. Just thought you might want to know."

She wheeled Stephanie toward a Subaru with a mirror ball swinging from its rearview mirror, and Moony wondered what Dotty was doing here at three in the morning and whether she was the nun in question.

Perry watched her go. "See? This place is already more interesting than I thought."

The key fit the lock to unit 150. The roll-up door opened to reveal filing cabinets, boxes of hard drives, and three rows of identical metal briefcases. He opened the nearest filing cabinet. The top drawer was labeled "Innovations in Hospitality LLC— Nebraska." Inside, Moony found incorporation documents for what appeared to be a chain of motels that he guessed existed only on paper. Bank statements showed regular deposits from "Friendship Column Enterprises" and "Golden Show Wellness Solutions."

The second drawer: "Prairie Communion Fellowship." Articles of incorporation for a religious organization with tax-exempt status. Donation records from dozens of names, each giving amounts just under the reporting threshold.

Perry whistled. "Is this what I think it is?"

"You should tell me what you think it is."

"I think it's records belonging to one of the world's most boring crime syndicates."

The third drawer made Moony's stomach drop. Passport applications, all with different names but subtle variations of the same few faces. Birth certificates from hospitals that had closed in the 1980s. Social Security cards for people born in towns that no longer existed.

Abel Proust-Johns. Born 1983, Angel Chorus, Nebraska (town dissolved 1987). Parents: Michael and Sarah Proust-Johns (deceased, no records). SSN issued 2001.

Magdalena Cross. Born 1985, Deadman Falls, Wyoming (town evacuated 1989, Superfund site). Homeschooled. First official record: library card, Denver Public Library, 2003.

Each identity came with a complete history—school records, employment, addresses.

"These are like . . ." Perry picked up a file. "What? Background people with whole lives that never happened."

"Ghost citizens," Moony said.

"I like 'background people.'"

At the bottom of the drawer, a manila envelope marked "Active—Do Not Destroy." Inside, three driver's licenses with the same photo but different names, different states, different birth dates.

Moony thought he understood now. The Gypsy had needed the storage facility to be owned by someone with credentials that would pass any scrutiny. But he was supposed to go through proper channels, get introduced to her keeper of the threshold, who'd ensure he never knew what he was storing and that he'd never set foot in the place.

By buying the facility directly, he'd burned through her plan. Now he owned evidence that was valuable but also incriminating as he had no plausible deniability. She'd made sure of it by actually giving him the key to the unit. She'd forced him across the line. It would have been fine if he had no idea what was in these units. She just needed him to own them. To be the clean name on the paperwork when questions got asked.

This was what happened when you spent years waiting to become important. In another version of this story, he would have called the FBI. In this version, he became complicit. Both versions end the same way.

Moony closed the filing cabinet, walked out, and locked the unit.

"The beautiful thing about tools," Perry said, pulling onto the street, "is that when something breaks, you fix it and move on. No need to store broken things forever."

❖ ❖ ❖

Deb's phone played whale sounds. She was in Sod Hill apartment P314, the unit they'd briefly considered renting as "bathroom optional" after a prior tenant had poured concrete down the toilet. They decided to wait until Q215 opened up to combine them. For now, it was Deb's private retreat. It was directly adjacent to Moony's, and she could hear the bass from video games through the wall.

She rolled off the mattress. The TV, always on mute, showed an infomercial for a device that scrambled eggs inside their shells. "My life has never been the same," someone said. "Best decision I've ever made."

Deb thought about all the other decisions that person might have made. Whether they were in a relationship, the various career choices they'd navigated. Life-changing trips they might have gone on. Other, more significant purchases they might have made. Whether they'd decided to have children and what their children might feel about their parent saying such a thing.

Just an hour earlier, she'd made a significant decision of her own.

Deb's first husband, Steele, had shown up at Sod Hill on a Tuesday, driving a Lexus with dealer plates and wearing the same

❖ 134 ❖

cologne that had made an impression on her at nineteen. She'd met him in the parking lot, standing by the dumpsters where someone had abandoned a massage chair that might have been used as target practice.

"You look incredible," Steele said, reaching for her waist. He had a southern accent so thick it found ways of inserting extra syllables into the vowel transitions in many words.

She stepped back. "Stop." She pulled out the Polaroid camera she'd been carrying everywhere lately. "Stand right there."

"What?"

"Just stand there. By that old piece of junk."

The camera made the familiar winding whir, and the flashbulb went off despite the broad daylight. Steele stood there with his hands doing that thing where he clearly wanted to put them in his pockets, but his pants were too tight to do so in any way that seemed natural.

The image materialized: a stocky man in a tight polo shirt standing next to garbage.

"This is how I want to remember you," she said, pocketing the photo.

"Deb—" he said, pronouncing it *Day-ub*.

"I've been your escape hatch for twenty-four years, Steele. Every time Sharon gets too real, every time your life feels too small, you show up here like I'm some kind of fun rest stop between your actual life and whatever you think you want."

"You don't mean that."

She laughed, and it surprised her how obviously joyful it sounded. "I'm done being your excuse, honey. Find someone else to not quite commit to."

He looked at his hands, then at her, then at the massage chair.

"Go home, Steele. For once in your life, go all the way home."

Back in P314, she looked at the Polaroid before taping it to the wall of the no-toilet apartment next to her vision board. Steele by the dumpster, already fading. She saw on the vision board representations of many things she'd already attained: yoga teacher training in Sedona, Reiki certification, the tantric workshop where an elderly woman named Barb told her that her biggest spiritual awakening would come "in advanced years, involving water and a stranger."

On the floor, her library: *Attached: The New Science of Adult Attachment*, *The Ethical Slut*, *The Multi-Orgasmic Woman*, all dog eared and annotated. The TV switched to an infomercial for a ladder that could hold five hundred pounds. "Built for real life," the announcer promised.

❖ ❖ ❖

Perry looked into Moony's bathroom mirror, straightening his bow tie.

Moony had not yet begun to dress. He entertained himself with *Medal of Honor* for Xbox 360. He believed that, ever since he had gotten sick from the caveman's apricot water, he had improved at game playing.

"Hey, asshole!" said Perry. "Get off your ass." He grinned at Moony and, to the tune of *Auld Lang Syne*, clapped and sang the words "I only look after number one," over and over again.

A knock on the door.

Deb was not an expected guest, though she carried a bottle of wine and was dressed seductively.

"Oh God . . ." said Perry, guilty as Lassie eating the family rib eye. There he stood, dressed to kill with a shiny belt buckle, sporting the bad posture of a person who was caught offending a loved one.

"Perry!" said Deb. She actually dropped the wine bottle. Then she thought of a story. "I've been looking for you. But you're dressed already. I thought you were going to stand me up."

Perry did not like to lie. He was not good at it. "Moony and I are going on a double date tonight."

From the other room, Moony whistled, and there was the sound of detonation from a video game.

"You didn't tell me it was going to be a double." Deb had apparently not caught on. Many times, when people are busy weaving their own lies, their attention toward other people is not very astute.

"Deb, there is a lady waiting for me at the restaurant. I will explain everything later. If you want me to be exclusive, then I guess we need to have a bigger conversation." Perry stood there looking like a man who'd just announced he was thinking about jumping off a bridge, waiting to see if anyone would talk him down or hand him a parachute. "About, you know . . . " He gestured vaguely between himself and Deb, then toward Moony's apartment, where the sounds of simulated warfare continued unabated. "About what we are. What that is. Whether we're . . ." He made another helpless gesture that encompassed their entire complicated arrangement.

"Oh," Deb said. She looked at Moony. There he stood, not shrugging, not defending her, not doing anything for anyone. "Perry, sweetheart, if I wanted us to be exclusive, don't you think I would have mentioned it by now?"

For just a moment, she looked like a woman who'd been practicing this exact conversation in her head for weeks, rehearsing the perfect response that would make her seem unaffected, only to discover that saying the words out loud felt different than she'd imagined. Then she stormed downstairs, muttering something about white wine being better than red anyway.

"Shall we?" said Moony, sporting the same clothes he slept in, which, truth be told, were more expensive than Perry's outfit.

The two men left Moony's apartment and stepped into the cold. They approached Moony's car across the parking lot.

A tall blonde woman stormed up like a Viking in high heels.

Perry glanced at Moony, hoping he would be allowed to speak with her.

Moony's mother. She looked like someone who had an agenda.

In fact, today's entry in her daily planner, which featured stationary that had Get drunk and: at the beginning of each to-do list, read:

Get drunk and fire the tax attorney.

Facial appointment Tuli's Spa 11:30

Get drunk and give Dan his gramps's watch and lucky salmon tie

The stationery ended with *Get drunk and get on with it.*

❖ ❖ ❖

"You've been a stranger," said Moony's mother.

They briefly, briskly hugged.

She towered above most men in ways that suggested witnessing a power they usually had to pay to see, an authority manifest in strippers when they enjoyed their occupation.

"Joanna, meet my friend. Perry, Joanna, Joanna, Perry."

"Hi, nice to meet you."

"You, too."

Perry looked around, asking "Wasn't Celia here, or where is she?" He fumbled to put on his Oakley sunglasses and shake hands at the same time and said to Joanna "We were just off to a business meeting."

Moony corrected, "No, we weren't. We have a double date scheduled."

"Right. The truth."

They gave each other a fist pump.

"We're on our way to pick up our dates for dinner," Moony said.

"I'm hungry. Haven't eaten in days it feels like," said Joanna. She put her hands on her abdomen. Yes, she, too, had a six-pack.

"Pick something up from the Thai place a block down." Moony pointed north, then south.

"I think she'd like to go with us."

"Take my house key and eat my leftovers," said Moony. "I've got some old doughnuts or whatever."

"Hop in," said Joanna, "I'll ferry you to your dates."

"Out of the question. And as you can see, I have my own car," said Moony.

"Your tire is flat," said Joanna.

Moony looked. Damn, it sure was.

"There's time to fix it."

They were already late.

In heels, Joanna tromped toward her Escalade. Perry followed in eager conversation with her. They were speaking about just what a "bacon strip" was and wasn't.

The car's interior smelled like cigars. Joanna relished cigars with the best of any obese Central American businessman from the 1970s.

"Big Train" by Mike Watt played on the stereo.

In the back seat, Perry lit a cigarette.

"So where do these broads live?" was all Joanna said for the duration of the drive. Other than that, she gave curt nods that suggested she had heard and/or considered what was being said.

Perry listened to the lyrics and moved his head to the music.

Moony gave precise directions, never saying more than necessary. He looked out the window at the parts of town that did not decorate themselves because snow often would. They drove past a building with a sign reading David Building. He coveted the award-winning anonymity in these places. Now back in the toxic embrace of his family, he wondered if he'd be heading toward that sort of future. He envisioned himself being installed in some operational role at the holding company in Ecuador, the meetings he'd take, the cafes he'd frequent.

Parked at a stoplight, he stared intently at a mustached bum. The bum looked honest, Moony thought, and pulled his face into an expression that mimicked that of the man on the street.

At the green light, their car drove away.

In a few minutes, Celia and Yvonne both sat in the back seat, Perry in between them. Yvonne wore a swishy black dress, and Celia sported a pair of vintage jeans and a clever T-shirt advertising a nonexistent surfboard company. It read "I Ride Moony's Longboard."

Celia and Yvonne, it turns out, had previously met and complimented each other's clothes at the Frog House's screening of *King Kong*, so while in Joanna's car, they spoke of each other's clothes this time and their opinions of *King Kong*.

The music on the stereo now was the Velvet Underground.

Yvonne asked Joanna to turn the volume down, but Joanna didn't hear.

She didn't ask again.

❖ ❖ ❖

To the candlelit table in Littleton's classiest Italian restaurant, the waiter brought a fifth chair to squeeze in between Moony and Celia.

Joanna asked if smoking was allowed.

The waiter said it was not.

"For now, I'll have a mint gelato, please."

"Ah, so you're ready to order?"

Contrary to the restaurant's name, which consisted of Italian words, the menu's assortment of cuisine did not appear preferential to any region.

"He'll have the filet mignon," said Celia, ordering for Moony.

She looked to Joanna, who said, "Yes, sounds good," to get her to look away.

Celia got fries and ate half of them.

Yvonne munched some of her salad in between looks around at the other people at the restaurant.

Devouring his medium steak, Moony said "Mmm, this is very good," and believed it since he was a sucker for Celia.

Having ordered a "Cowboy Burger," Perry was true to his tastes; his meal tasted the best.

No one talked for a while. Moony sat on his hands when he finished eating. When the waiter returned, Joanna asked to see a menu.

Yvonne motioned toward a dark woman sipping wine at a corner table. "She doesn't look away."

Moony suspected the woman had something to do with the Gypsy. The resemblance was strong—the same angular cheekbones that caught shadow like a Renaissance painting, the same way of holding her head as if balancing a crown. Her hair, though styled in tight curls, was capable of moving independently of any breeze, as if it wasn't sure if it should be somewhere else.

"Probably unwise to get involved with that woman," said Moony.

"What business is this you're getting into?" asked Joanna.

"Sales," answered Celia. Moony said thanks to her by sighing with relief.

Perry asked Yvonne what she liked to do in her free time.

"Oh. Whatever, really." Entranced, she watched the woman finish her wine.

"Was the ice cream good?" asked Moony.

"I'm ready for more wine, to be perfectly honest."

"Oh, me, too," said Celia.

Joanna called the server.

"Ah, I'll have this." She pointed at random. "I adore that one." She looked around the table, "What does that selection say about who I am? Any judgers?"

"I used to be a professional wine taster," said Moony, "and your choice was first rate."

"Ah? Let me guess—was that during your ... exploratory phase?" said Joanna, examining her wine glass with theatrical interest. "I seem to recall you had quite a few of those. Oenology, was it? Or was that the month you were going to be a pilot?" She smiled sweetly. "So hard to keep track. I do hope you're finding your path, dear. Sometimes it takes . . . time."

"I'll have a guess, too. That was when you lived abroad?" said Perry, lips painted purple from wine.

The woman glided by the table, on her way handing Moony a pair of lorgnettes. She said, "Just as two individuals join in love and union, we have bonds with spirits of other dimensions and times."

"That was your client?" Joanna asked. "My dear, as long as we're handing out gifts, I brought you this." She handed Moony a small box. Inside was a Rolex. "You said you lost yours, so I couldn't resist."

"I sometimes make collages," said Yvonne, delayed. They looked at her. Celia touched Yvonne's shoulder.

"I like collages, too, dear."

Moony said, "Deb stole my watch, actually. But thank you so much for this. It's fantastic."

"Who's Deb?" asked Joanna.

"Perry's fiancée," Moony answered.

"Oh?" said Yvonne, eyeing Perry. "You're engaged?"

Perry prepared a mental outline of his relationship troubles with Deb. To smooth things over, Joanna asked Celia what her family did.

"I'm an orphan."

Joanna laughed a single *ha*. "Little orphan Celia."

Celia stared at her napkin; it was floral and did nothing but remain stationary.

Joanna looked down at the napkin, too. "You were serious. Well. You're welcome in my home any time. Ignore all the gentleman callers. Dan Senior is so very busy, see."

"What a shame," said Perry. The way he looked at Joanna distracted her for a moment.

"Shames ... Oh. My husband, where to start. Have you ever heard of the stamp test?" Joanna asked.

"Stamp test?" Celia inquired.

"Take a few stamps, depending on girth, wrap them around the cock, stick them to each other. If morning comes and the stamps are still sealed to each other—no busting the seal, no proof of morning wood—then it's a physical problem. Three nights in a row to make sure. This isn't a clinical thing, of course. I may have invented it, but you think it's credible, no? By the second night he was so nervous, I can't imagine he could have slept, let alone sprouted any oak trees," Joanna confessed, looking back at Perry, "The poor snoring asshole. Moony, the watch was Thurman Jr.'s. I have a tie of his as well. You've been through a lot, handling your sister's mistake. It's in the glove box. The tie, not the mistake."

The statement hit Moony in the chest. "Don't call it a mistake."

"Beg pardon? Should I ask your advice on what to call it? A full-term miscarriage?"

"Why do you have to always be like this?"

"I'd like you to be more specific, if you can." Joanne reached in her pocket and brought out a notepad, then put it back. She locked eyes with him. For just a moment, her jaw tightened, and Moony noticed that she pressed her tongue against the inside of her cheek—a tell of hers he recognized. She'd do it whenever she was forcing herself to say something she didn't have full conviction of, her neck muscles straining as if the words were fighting to stay unspoken. She was performing confidence while actually in doubt, and beneath her cutting remarks lay something she couldn't afford to expose. Moony hoped that it was guilt over

Yvette or worse—the truth that she had no idea how to be a mother to her remaining adult children.

He couldn't let go of his anger. "What the hell do you expect me to do, stuck in some shit place in the suburbs with a bunch of weirdos and petty addicts?"

"Dan, dear, you wanted to go there."

"I wanted to be where you wouldn't have your fingers on the scales of my life."

"Be careful what you wish for."

"Stop assuming I need your help."

In Moony's mind, the Gypsy's proposition kept returning like one of those spinning newspapers in old movies—the kind that whirl toward the camera before stopping on a headline: Russian Money Buys American Real Estate. Not the flashy Manhattan penthouses that drew attention, but storage units, strip malls, apartment complexes: places where cash could sit and appreciate while their owners dealt with sanctions, investigations, or the not-so-occasional assassination attempt back home.

The beauty of it was the banality. Who tracked the ownership of a dozen scattered properties when they were buried under layers of LLCs and management companies? The oligarchs understood what his father had taught him: the best power was the kind no one could see.

And now he was getting in on the action.

He'd need escape routes, of course. The family vineyard in Spain was a downright fortress, but that was too obvious. Maybe something in Croatia—the Balkans were useful for disappearing. A boat registration in the Bahamas. A condo in Dubai, where extradition was complicated. Just in case things went sideways.

He'd get to the family business when he felt like it. When they'd earned his attention again. When they stopped treating him like a sleeper asset gathering dust in suburban Denver.

His father would have called this "going native," the way assets sometimes forgot their purpose and started believing their cover stories. But Moony wondered if maybe the opposite was true—maybe he'd been living the cover story his whole life, and this—playing old video games and road tripping with his landlord—was his real life.

He thought of Yvette again, how she'd tried to explain it to him. "I want to be my own person," she'd said. At the time, he'd thought she meant she wanted to be nobody. Now he understood that she wanted to be somebody, just not the somebody their family had designed.

Yvonne looked deep into Perry's eyes. "You have so many beautiful colors in your eyes," she said.

"My eyes are brown."

"But there's green in there, too, around the edges." Yvonne's former boyfriend had green eyes.

"What a riot," said Joanna, at Yvonne.

"A party!" said Celia.

At the mention of a party, Moony offered some new information to pull the dinner vibe out of the toilet. "I used to throw parties whenever for whoever wanted to come. I remember this time we had to clear out the whole floor of the hotel because someone's friend brought a tiger cub, and the tiger's owner was nowhere to be found. While they called and were waiting on some zookeeper to show up, nature called for me, and I opened the door of the bathroom to find her in there. She was pouncing at shadows in the empty jacuzzi, perfectly unaware and entertaining herself."

"Did you end up using the bathroom?" Perry asked.

"When you have to go, you have to go," Moony said. "The tiger was a real kitten. She could have easily killed me. But she was a sweetheart. I took her home for a while and ended up sending her to some place or other where she could have a nature-like environment. Not a zoo. Not some goddamn cage. But not necessarily the wild because she was pals with people. Domesticating animals ruins them for nature."

"That's probably the most interesting bathroom story I've ever heard," said Yvonne to Joanna. "And as long as we're telling penis stories and bathroom tales at the dinner table, I should share a bit of advice from my older brother, coincidentally also named Dan. He once told me that there were three ways of hanging toilet paper on the roll."

"Dan, yes. Dan is a gentleman's name," Joanna answered, then took a long drink of wine, using a bit of the tip of her tongue to guide the glass, her lips breathing an O around the red wine.

"The right way, the wrong way, and bachelor style."

Perry laughed and said "bachelor style" to himself so he would remember the term later.

As they left the restaurant, Moony decided to test something. He told his mother that, although he was very busy with his own work, he didn't understand why the family hadn't been in contact. He watched her face, trying to determine if her response would mean they'd been monitoring him from a distance–and if so, whether as concerned parents or as handlers letting an asset develop in the field.

"Work? At your opera or wherever? Your kids aren't going to worry about inheritance tax, are they?"

Yvonne chimed in. "Picasso's children paid off their inheritance tax with more artwork. The government opened up a museum of that stuff in a big house."

"Let's stop by McDonald's." Joanna eyed Perry. "I could be down for a burger. Down, down, down."

Moony slapped his forehead.

"Dan, honey, remember to call AAA to fix your tire," Joanna said as they got into her Escalade. A bumper sticker on it read GUN CONTROL MEANS USING BOTH HANDS. She didn't own a gun, but she liked to use both hands.

Moony didn't feel like calling. He decided the manufacturer should have placed sensors in the car so whenever something went wrong mechanically, the sensor would go off and trigger the mechanic to arrive. The car would also need a tracking device in it, of course, so the vehicle-fixing person could locate it.

Joanna chewed her lip. Perry watched her from the passenger seat.

"Let's go to that art show tomorrow. The one Perry is putting on," Joanna said to Moony.

He hadn't heard of it.

It was to be held at the bank a few blocks from Sod Hill. Perry was good friends with the owners. They gave him the key to the front door and security codes, and he pledged to bring in fifty new customers in a year's time. So far, he had brought in seventeen. Art was donated by residents. The event was called the Bi-Weekly Whitecomb Art Fair.

"A funeral might have been really nice," said Joanna with a mouthful of cheeseburger. "Lots of people would show, wonderful reception. Open casket, she'd look lovely in there." Joanna had never been taught how to respond to tragedy.

"Is it a long drive to your hotel?" Perry asked.

Yvonne, Celia, and Moony could only hear Joanna's drum and bass music: Dieselboy.

"Beg your pardon?"

"Can I interest you in a nightcap?"

She offered him the hamburger. "Do you want the rest of this?"

He shook his shaggy head. "Sleep in my bed."

As if it had rung, she picked up her cell phone and dialed her assistant, letting her know she wouldn't be coming home.

Perry received a very nice kiss goodbye from Yvonne when she was dropped off.

On the Escalade's stereo now was Sonic Youth's "One Hundred Percent."

Sitting in the back seat, Moony could not make out the conversation between Joanna and Perry, but the two seemed charmed with each other.

Stephen Lloyd Webber

❖ ❖ ❖

When they returned to Sod Hill, they could see in the orange street lights that Shadrack and Heath were having a row.

Shadrack was wearing Heath's clothes, threatening to slide down the snowy hill using the God pot as a sled.

"You said you were just going to look into it!" Heath said, rock in hand.

Shadrack laughed a happy demon laugh. "I get better reception up here!" He put the pot on his head.

Heath threw the stone as hard as he could—it dented the pot and knocked Shadrack over with a sound like a church bell splitting. Shadrack tossed the pot down the hill and ran at Heath, who was already entering Moony's apartment to hide out.

When Moony got there, he asked Heath if he wanted any of Celia's leftover french fries. Heath said yes, and Moony plopped the takeout box on the coffee table.

Heath sat down on the couch, running his tongue across his dentures and contemplating the future. This was the last time he sat down on Moony's couch.

"Shadrack put a potato in your tailpipe, but you never drove, so it just shriveled and fell out."

Heath and Moony made conversation that, within hours, neither would remember the details of. But they decided to see each other for the true sovereign beings they were, which meant that they were able to get actual glimpses of each other's humanity. For people who share even the remotest of values, that's all it ever really takes.

Exhausted, Moony went to bed.

In the middle of the night, Heath stood in the bedroom doorway holding his rock friend and watched Moony sleep face down on his pillow, as if life had given him an insurmountable burden, or at least as if he had yet to learn how to shoulder one.

◆ ◆ ◆

The Bi-Weekly Whitecomb Art Fair began at nine the next day. A few bank customers came and went, glad to have the extended hours. Some patrons slowed their walk to a museum pace to take in the paintings, occasionally taking a cookie as well.

The fish tank Mr. Perry Whitecomb had brought in for the occasion sat on an untrustworthy table designed by a Sod Hill tenant. It was five feet tall and had three legs. The artist comforted Perry by explaining that three legs formed a pyramid and would prove to be much more stable than a table with four legs. The more basic the shape, he said, the stronger the structure. But since the fish tank weighed more than either could guess and contained jellyfish, Perry was nervous it would collapse. Interesting note: the table was not designed to support any weight at all.

"I just love this piece," said Joanna, pointing at a mostly green painting. "Is it for sale?"

Moony wasn't a person who understood art. But seeing his mother regard the painting, he felt encouraged to try. After some dull moments spent deciphering it, he got the impression something canine lurked behind the canvas, an opaque green window. He didn't wonder why. Above all, he just wanted something like a magic eye painting to really exist.

Perry had neglected to work out details of sale possibilities with the artists. No prices had been set. He mentioned this since he had nothing to hide.

Joanna laughed, charmed. She offered to pay whatever the artist asked for the piece: "But don't you tell them I said that. Just find out what their price is, would you?"

Because Joanna was dressed in yellow and rust, colors that complimented the bank's décor, many patrons assumed Joanna was an artist. They asked her which pieces were hers. Alas, she would say, none of them, not unless she could buy them. She released an enchanting laugh, its edges textured beautifully by the recreational smoking she did. She was an avid drinker of licorice tea, and it kept her voice high priced and intact.

Joanna had a way of standing near Moony that made him forget any need to represent himself. In this moment, he was unable to access his near-universal feelings of resentment and self-loathing—or his suspicion that the woman he remembered from early childhood had looked different, acted different. Families like his replaced things all the time: cars, houses, inconvenient details. Why not mothers? He was happy to be alive. Sometimes, he could never be happier.

Moony, not thinking, said the part about being happy aloud.

Joanna turned to him. "Every up has a down."

The table, motivated by an unseen force, rumbled under the burden of the aquarium. *Perhaps the helium balloons tied to it will help*, thought Perry—they couldn't hurt.

Moony did a double take as he watched yet another woman who bore some resemblance to the Gypsy exit the bank, alone. He moved a step or two toward the door to inquire about her presence, but no further. There were no security guards at the bank today.

Some sort of businessman engaged himself in conversation with Joanna. "I'm in real estate," he said since everyone in suburban Denver those days was in real estate. He might have been flirting.

Spotting his wedding band, she intimidated him into moving elsewhere. In her mysterious way, she motivated some men to become more. This motivation, instigated spontaneously in this man, would last a full two weeks, unsupported by any other event, and he came to treat his wife a little better for the remaining seven years of their marriage.

A woman approached Moony. "What a nice collection of art," she said.

"I'm in town for a funeral," Moony said. The woman walked away with a respectful smile.

Standing next to the jellyfish, Joanna became the center of attention at the art show. She crafted entrancing falsities about the artist of the green painting. "We said goodbye to each other in Ireland, and that was it."

"Oh, how lovely!" gasped a patron in response.

"Yes, I guess you could say that the portrait is of the mood between us. Green is the color of jealousy, you know. Envy, too, but also of beginnings—oh, we were so young." She looked away and was bored.

Heath walked from painting to painting, whispering to his rock about some of the newest mysteries of science. "Oh, how remarkable!" said another patron, believing Heath was a piece of performance art.

Joanna leaned against the table, and it tumbled. Hundreds of gallons of water spilled. Jellyfish merged with commercial carpet. Patrons and customers wailed and gasped.

A few seconds later, a person said, "Oh my God!"

Joanna yelled, "My jellyfish!" even though they were not her jellyfish.

Perry ran to the bathroom for paper towels.

Bystanders stood by.

Bank employees searched for the security guard.

Moony grabbed his mother's wrist as if she were a drunk teenager and escorted her to the car. She laughed guiltily and loud.

Inside the bank, a teller who had decided it was her responsibility to at least attempt to pursue the guilty party slipped on the wet tile floor and landed face first on a helpless jellyfish, which promptly wrapped itself around her skin as if in defense.

Perry called an ambulance.

❖ ❖ ❖

Joanna stared at Moony's jaw as he drove, considering slapping his face for extricating her without her consent, but the car seat was comfortable. There was some salt water on her feet, which she encouraged to soak into and ruin her shoes.

"Why are you here? Why are you lurking around me?" Moony asked.

"Lurking? I'm your mother. Mothers don't lurk, they ... supervise from a distance."

"Don't tell me it's because you're falling for Perry."

"Perry is a wonderful and surprising man. But I'm here because you're all I have left that isn't trying to be Dan Senior and his stupid contracts. Alex is—never mind. Just drive."

Moony looked over at her, but by that time, she'd recovered, and her face was inscrutable. She rubbed a small red welt on her wrist where a jellyfish tentacle had grazed her.

"To the shoe store."

His jaw clenched and released. He could feel his mother staring at him.

"Daniel."

"Hmm?"

"I need to ask you something, and I need you to answer honestly."

"Hmm."

"Are you taking anything? Or have you stopped taking something you should be taking?"

He shook his head. "My training has conditioned me to endure the effects of many chemicals."

Joanna pursed her lips, held her breath for a long time, then exhaled carefully.

"Your father and I discussed this when you moved to that place. We thought—a change of scenery, some time away, maybe that's helpful. But if you're ..." She searched for the word. "If you're feeling . . . lost or something, we can get you help."

"A good cover requires commitment."

"That's the language, Daniel. That's the language. We need you to rein that in."

Moony gave a slow nod, either understanding or moving deeper into not understanding. "It won't happen again."

"People who are fine don't move into golf-themed apartment complexes and play Xbox for eighteen hours a day."

"It's Super Nintendo, and it's only a few hours, and I'm *perfectly operational*." He smiled the way Mister Rogers might, if Mister Rogers happened to be suppressing a whole universe of experience. "That was a great art show."

A better man would have known what to do with everything he was trying to navigate. He'd already be two steps ahead with the Gypsy's opportunity or else have slammed the door in her face. Now he had a personal link to someone else's money laundering and identity farming operation. She would no doubt soon dangle a new mystery in front of him, keep him occupied. He hated feeling downstream of everyone and everything, the effect of someone else's cause.

Joanna, for her part, seemed content that she had said her bit, and he had heard her. She sent Perry a text message saying she would be spending her afternoon at Saks Fifth Avenue teasing the shoes.

"Oh yes," she said, queenly. She paused. "I really did like the green one. The sky is very pretty today. Blah blah blah."

In response, Moony appreciated the blue beauty of the empty sky. He had inherited her ability to select what would affect her.

He lit a cigarette.

His mother's face showed the beginnings of becoming aghast. "It's as if you're living on the street. You're smoking cigarettes in my car." She decided she couldn't tolerate the smell of cigarettes anymore.

Moony considered living on the street. "I've been thinking about travel. To Europe," he lied.

"There's nothing wrong with that. Stay in the Cannes apartment."

Moony decided to run a red light since the way was clear.

"Stay with the Langs in Germany. They have a place right there on the Rhein. Freiburg near the Black Forest maybe." She thought for a moment. "I remember when we stayed there—you were eight. You were convinced the place was overrun with tarantulas. Ah, you were so afraid of spiders."

He blew smoke in her direction.

❖ ❖ ❖

Perry, toweling a jellyfish off his cowboy boot, worked with several bank employees to assess and attempt to remedy the water damage to the bank.

He spoke on the phone with a professional. "These are cement floors and a cement foundation, correct?" The conversation had the seriousness of those foundations. "The tile adhesive won't be corroded with the salt water, will it? . . . Well, that's good. At least that means 'the salinity will discourage mold growth,'" he repeated to the bank manager, who was red in the face.

◆ ◆ ◆

The Saks Fifth Avenue store in Denver's Cherry Creek mall bustled with Valentine's Day shoppers. Moony and his mother browsed the shoe section.

Karisma, a sales associate who was astoundingly overweight and enormously cheerful, helped Joanna feel flirtatious toward the ordinary-looking expensive shoes: "The gold buttons on these look quite marvelous." "Yes, quite enjoyable." "Black goes with everything. It does; it really does," et cetera.

Across the atrium, through the glass storefront of another shop, Moony spotted a familiar silhouette. Celia—alone, but looking tousled in that amorous way he recognized instantly and didn't like. Their eyes met across the distance. A moment of dread passed between them, then she forced a smile.

Joanna kept laughing, Dior shoes in hand.

Moony excused himself and walked into the sounds of the mall atrium—the echo of footsteps on marble, the distant waterfall feature, conversations bleeding together. Celia met him halfway, running her hands over her clothing as if to smooth something out.

"Why do you smell like Italian food?" he asked.

"Oh, I—I made a big pot of spaghetti. Is there some place we can talk?"

Moony didn't move.

Back in Saks, Joanna had decided to get the heels. She liked the square of gold on the front of the shoe. They were the same as a month's rent at Sod Hill.

"These shoes are on sale, actually," Karisma said.

Joanna looked as if she didn't want anyone to overhear. "Oh, that's good," she responded.

Karisma went to the back room to get the shoes and returned with a sad face. "We don't have any in your size. I'm so sorry."

"Tell me," Moony said to Celia, already disappointed. Somewhere in him, he recognized a cliché, but it still hurt.

Celia sighed. "I hooked up with someone else."

It hit him like a knife in the chest.

"I'm sorry. I'm so sorry. It was really nothing. It wasn't even—I want to be with you. It's just—it's sort of complicated," she said, looking away. A sliver of light in the atrium arched down the curve of her neck. She kissed him.

He was full of rage. He loved her. He hated how he felt. He wasn't supposed to let something like this happen to him. They kissed some more. They could be so right for each other. He needed to make her understand.

She glanced around, then pulled him by the wrist toward a service corridor marked EMPLOYEES ONLY. He followed without resistance, past a cleaning cart and stacked boxes, through a heavy door that deposited them into what turned out to be Saks' back stockroom.

Celia led him deeper into the maze of shelving until they found a clearing among towers of shoeboxes.

To herself, she whispered, "This is so stupid." She wanted to feel depraved, so she figured she should get on her knees, and that would be a good way to start things.

He told her to get up. She wouldn't look him in the eyes. *Fine*, he decided, *have it your way.*

Karisma led Joanna into the back room. They heard it before they saw. The two women froze—neither wanted to confront what was happening, but they couldn't ignore it.

Joanna placed her hand over her mouth, almost chuckling.

Karisma stepped back as one confronted with a sudden wildfire, her face contorting with awe.

"Oh—Oh—" she stammered, her voice unrecognizable from the bubbly tone she'd used moments before. She made a strangled noise and backed flat against the wall.

Celia, caught in the act, didn't cower. Instead, she straightened up, eyes flashing. "What? You don't have an internet connection? No sense of curiosity?"

"This is a place of business!" Karisma hissed, finding her voice. She gestured at Joanna. "People try on footwear here!"

Joanna, who moments earlier had been stifling laughter, rearranged her features and nodded solemnly, as if she too were a victim of this trespass against retail decorum.

"Yeah, well, we were trying something on, too," Celia shot back.

The commotion drew the attention of a manager, who approached from behind Karisma. Her eyes widened at the scene before her.

"What is going on here?" she demanded.

Moony, strategically positioned behind a stack of expensive shoeboxes, raised his hands. "Let's all take a breath."

"I will not take a breath!" the manager snapped. "Security is on their way. This is completely unacceptable behavior in an establishment of footwear!"

Celia's face flushed with anger. "Oh, so now we need security? For what? You unsexed muggles call affection between consenting adults a security issue?"

Joanna's amusement was unconcealed once more. "Well," she said, her voice dropping to that icy register Moony had grown up with. She turned to Karisma. "I'll take my business elsewhere. Somewhere with more . . . private fitting rooms."

With that parting shot, she glided out, leaving a chill in her wake.

Moony zipped up and stepped forward. "There's been a misunderstanding," he said to the entire room. "We're leaving now. No need for security or further discussion."

"Then go," the manager said.

Celia grabbed her purse, glaring at everyone. "This place is ridiculous anyway." She stormed out, not waiting for Moony.

Moony sat down on the stack of shoeboxes for a while, wondering what Celia needed that she couldn't get from him or Deb. The door swung shut behind her, and he felt something twist in his chest. He felt only the weight of being, once again, the person left behind while someone else moved forward.

With everyone else in his party gone, neither Karisma nor the manager paid him any mind.

Certain that he was alone—truly alone, in the way only someone surrounded by thousands of dollars' worth of unworn shoes can be—he departed.

❖ ❖ ❖

Moony called a driver and had the driver drop him off at the bank.

"It's you again," said a teller.

"Listen, I'm sorry about what happened."

She looked entirely confused. "It's not your fault. Perry warned us about the jellyfish idea, but we thought it would look nice, so we went for it. The woman who got stung in the face, it was actually her idea. The jellyfish was her idea, not the face stinging," the teller clarified.

The floor of the bank, draped in towels and taped off, reminded Moony of something. It wasn't déjà vu. He couldn't quite place it. His foot seemed to sink a little too far into the carpet. It welcomed him with an insidious squish.

"Are you OK?"

"Oh," said Moony. "Let me know if there's anything I can do, I guess."

The teller, Zelda, wrote her number down on a card. "If you're still feeling guilty for no reason"–she handed it to him–"I have a degree in psychology, actually. Maybe you need some counseling." She laughed.

There was a very attractive venom in her laugh. He took a half-step backward.

"I get off work in a few minutes. But only call me if you're feeling guilty already," she said. "Otherwise I don't know what we would talk about."

"Should I be terrified that I was raised to believe I'm at the center of the world no matter where I go?"

She laughed for no reason. "If that were literally true, I guess I'd be filled with spinning molten lava, and I'm afraid that's just not so."

He smiled, the carpet gazing up at him like an old acquaintance.

He left and walked four blocks back to Sod Hill. Standing at his door, he felt foreign to it and thought about knocking. Instead, he used the lobby phone to call Zelda.

❖ ❖ ❖

Moony reclined even more on Zelda's bean bag chair, pressing the back of his head into it to hear that squish sound. He was exceedingly inebriated. He thought, *"Very soon I am escaping all my troubles."*

She sat across from him, happy as a lark, naked as a jaybird, and high as a kite. She stared at her hands.

Moony began staring at his hands, musing about something Heath had told him at some point: "Because of the existence of intercellular space, your brain has infinite surface area; therefore, you can know everything."

Her living room was a cute rainforest full of fuzzy pink accessories: she had pink lampshades, frilly coasters, shag carpet picture frames, and penholders full of glitter-topped pens, yet somehow the room managed to look only slightly less than reasonably mature and sophisticated. Moony toyed with the idea of actually receiving some counseling from Zelda, but while he deliberated, she commented that it looked like he was crying—his face was all screwed up—so they got even higher, and he struck up a conversation.

"If you could go on a vacation someplace in Europe tomorrow, where would you want to go?"

"Ancient Prussia," she said.

"I was thinking someplace warm."

"France," she answered in an instant.

"Warmer."

"Modern Russia," she said.

"How about Turkey?"

"That's not in the European Union, is it?"

"We could drive around Boulder."

She lost interest, saying "You know when you go to the supermarket, and of those coffee beans are in different sacks?"

"Mmm?" asked Moony, wondering at the phrase Eurasia + Oneness = Horatio.

"Different companies and different regions, some of them fair trade, some Folgers? What if they all just mixed together, the packages dissolved into each other, then when we went to buy coffee we'd have things the way they really are. Instead of getting a fair price for an unfair trade, we'd get a semi-fair price for mixed beans."

Moony remembered his balcony flag from Portugal had fallen. Maybe that meant something.

"Portugal would be nice. I'll see if we can get a house on the coast somewhere. Do you want a coffee or something?"

"No way, not here. Not now. Not like this." She ran her fingers down the hem of her skirt, preparing to put it on.

She's weird, thought Moony. Using Zelda's computer, he looked up some information on travel to Portugal, thinking *What is intimacy, anyway?* He was pretty sure he was not good at it.

"The south part of Portugal looks nice. Oh, I think you'd love these people I know who have a house not too far away."

Zelda curled into a ball and decided to stay undressed. "Oh, we should go there." She mused about the times when she was a girl and loved to order things in the mail. She loved to get packages, and if the delivery was not on the expected date, she would obsess over not getting the package—not verbally, but to herself. She was able to project all the possibilities for her fulfillment onto the moments when she opened packages, gifts, presents. She would keep her mind on the mailbox all day—the mailman had no idea what he meant to her.

Four to six weeks was the perfect amount of time for waiting to receive a package since the first week she spent in anticipation, then she either distracted herself or otherwise moved on from it during the second or third week. Once she had fully moved on from her anxiety about the package, it surprised her one day in the mail, and she had never felt so good. The purity of the thing she received, its suchness, and that it was entirely external to her filled her with a threshold dose of guilt along with her actual joy from its presence.

Musing about going to Europe reminded her how so much was like that desire. Moony would be able to get them there tomorrow if that was what they decided to do. Looking at him, memorizing his looks, she wanted to become him; he was such a stranger.

"No, no Portugal. Let's do Spain."

"Are you sure? It's on a farm, this place I'm thinking of."

"I grew up on a farm," she said. "In Tennessee. It was all right."

"I didn't know that. Why didn't I know that?" Moony realized the familiarity he felt for her was misleading. *Her name is Zelda—that's a first*, he reminded himself, reflecting on their fucking. Her weight on him—assuredly not great—he had been enamored of it. The burden granted him the opposite feeling of floating; he felt grounded, himself. Freedom was not present, so there was no struggle to handle it. Even if he tried, he could not feel distant from her.

"You want to stop by the farm for a few days on the way to Spain?" he asked.

"Not really. We should go to Africa sometime."

"Africa is a whole continent," he said. *She's one of those idiots who doesn't know geography*, he thought, then shrugged it off. "Bring whatever you want. Beachwear, dresses. Pretty things. Are doilies clothing?"

"Have you ever thought about sending yourself a postcard when you're on vacation so you see what a nice time you had when you get back? A letter to yourself in the mail? I think I'll do that," Zelda said. "Did we use a condom?"

"Sort of. Why, are you horribly diseased?"

She shook her head, and that was good enough for Moony.

He kept forcing himself not to think of Celia.

"Send the package right before we leave, so you don't get it right away. Call in sick," Moony said, clicking around on her computer. "My family doctor can give you a note. You want to say you came down with rickets?"

"Above all else, I don't want to get sick. I can't go to Spain with you."

"Not now, but soon?"

"Very soon."

He didn't intend to ever speak with her again.

◆ ◆ ◆

Moony returned to a note on his door:

Joanna says your dad is ill. She also says it's nothing to worry about, but I'm not convinced. It's none of my business, but maybe you should visit? I have her new phone number if you want to call.

Perry

P.S. Get a phone.

"Heart disease will do that," Moony said, discovering that there was another note underneath Perry's. It was a series of numbers in no noticeable sequence. On the back of the note was Heath's handwriting: "these numbers spell similar things forward and in reverse." He threw the note into his trash can and stopped for a second. His apartment had the same carpet the bank did: white with vague clouds of red, brown, blue.

"Can you have a déjà vu in advance?" he asked.

Heath, eating cereal, perked up. He didn't have an answer, but the proposition blew his mind.

Moony put some stuff in his Berluti handbag. "I'm going to be gone for a few days. Hold down the fort for me."

❖ ❖ ❖

Moony and Celia, after some brief bickering, made it to the airport. There he stood at the check-in counter, watching the destination board with its list of options. Spain would be the obvious choice—safe, predictable, exactly what someone in his position would do. Run away to the family vineyard, drink wine, pretend nothing had changed. Charm both Celia and himself back into normalcy.

But Ecuador was in his mind like a loaded chamber.

His father was sick. What the old man needed even more than some illusion of affection or fealty from his progeny was . . . what? Alex would step up, of course. Alex, who understood the game, who'd been playing it since birth while Moony perfected *Double Dragon* combos.

There was a house in Ayampe, on the coast. His father had mentioned it exactly once, after three bourbons last Thanksgiving. This was his chance. Any trained dog could follow orders. But here he could seize the initiative for real. It was about proving you belonged at the table. That you could see an opening and take it without being told.

"Sir?" The ticket agent was waiting. "Your destination?"

Going to Ecuador would flip the switch. Set things in motion he couldn't control. But at least he'd be moving forward instead of sideways.

"Quito," he said. "Two tickets to Quito."

Celia sat her bags down in front of the counter. "Now it's you who smells funny."

"You want to finish telling me what the whole Saks thing was about?"

"We should forget about it."

"Exactly," he said.

"Two bags, ma'am?" said the ticket counter lady.

"Yes."

"All the way to Quito?"

"Yes."

"Have a nice trip."

"Thanks."

"Just the one bag for you, sir?"

"Yes."

"To Quito also?"

"Yes."

"Have a nice trip."

"Thanks." Moony resumed his thought. "I keep thinking about the time my brother was in the talent show, and he won, so I made fun of him at dinner till he cried."

"You did that?" she asked.

"Or when I had sex with six women in a night just to see if I could."

"I didn't know about that." She paused. "Was I one of them?"

He shook his head no, and he wasn't sure whether that disappointed her or not.

"You don't hear other people blabbing as if life were a confessional booth, do you?" asked Celia as they walked through a large crowd of Catholic school kids.

Moony felt embarrassed that they might have overheard but smiled at them as if he proudly wore devil horns.

❖ ❖ ❖

Heath, stepping out of his car, heard a tinny, subdued yipping coming from a closed dumpster. Inside a burgundy handbag was a scared puppy. He recognized the handbag as one he'd once owned and didn't remember throwing out.

"Is this my puppy?" he asked, cradling it. "Are there more of you in there?"

The dog, a young pit bull, didn't seem in a position to understand his question.

Heath glanced in the dumpster and, seeing only bags of trash, pressed his ear closer, hearing only the faint rustling-heartbeat sound of plastic whipping in the wind.

He took the dog upstairs, fed it, gave it water, and laid down to take a nap with it on the floor.

"It was such a good thing I got fired today so I could get my good parking space and hear you complaining."

The puppy was asleep.

"I'm going to feed you until you get six feet tall, and that's a good thing. Your fur is so brown, such a good thing." And Heath was asleep.

❖ ❖ ❖

Celia sat in her window seat and pulled down the shade.

"Why can't you leave the shade up?"

"Because it's sunny."

"Sunny is pretty."

"You sit here."

"I like the aisle."

"Then don't complain."

"I like the shade to be open because whoever sits in the window seat should like to look out. See the view."

"Right now the luggage guys out there are filling the plane with gas."

"The view later."

"I don't make you sit in the aisle seat any certain way."

"There's only one way to sit in an aisle seat—on your ass."

"With the shade down."

"The window seat with the shade pulled down is the worst possible seat because you're trapped in and have no view."

"There's the view. Of them filling gas."

"Of the clouds. See the pretty sky?"

Moony felt like he needed to pee. They were in first class, so he just got up and did his business. When he came back to find Celia crying, he didn't know what to do, so he held her. His arm around her, he felt something crumple like a plastic sack. He intruded into her pocket, curious. A baggie of cocaine.

"Who are you?"

"I never get searched." She smiled.

"That's insane—you couldn't get cocaine in Ecuador?"

Celia giggled. It was easy to laugh after a brief cry.

"Oh, whatever," Moony said, "Keep up the good work smuggling, I guess."

The overweight man beside them made the seat groan as his amorphous body twisted like a can of biscuit dough along his central axis, made the sort of face only a baby boomer could, and put on some Koss noise-canceling headphones.

Celia squeezed her nipples at the man and made a face.

❖ ❖ ❖

It wasn't easy to say how long the trip took, but Moony was pretty sure it took around fourteen hours. Considering they had been up all night packing and fussing like newlyweds over what to bring (he had forgotten his watch) and whether to splurge for private or just fly commercial, they were both able to get some rest on the plane. Moony had a few glasses of wine, but for some reason, he didn't want Celia to know he had been drinking. Would he seem less virile?

The weather in Ecuador was ridiculous in comparison to Denver. The sunshine alone was sufficient to cure diseases; it was so direct and serene. The landscape was startling in its simplicity: the dirt was red, the sky blue, and the beachside estate was yellow. The ocean view yielded everything to be hoped for in any horizon on planet Earth.

Moony fantasized about getting on the back of a horse again—he hadn't done that in years.

"Have you seen this bed?" Celia called from inside, her voice echoing off the stone floor and walls, sounding like the femme fatale in a noir film playing in a cheap underground theater.

"I have, actually," Moony said, entering the master bedroom. "Julieta and Roberto are friends of the family. They're—this is their place, officially. They're never here." He set down his bag. "They're painters, I think."

"Tired as I am, I'm going to lie on the beach anyway. If I fall asleep out there, don't let me stay long enough to burn."

"I'll go with you." They met each other's eyes.

For the rainy season in coastal Ecuador, you couldn't have asked for a better day on the beach. They spent a time in silence, holding hands, looking down at the long shadows cast by the sunset of a day they spent in the sky.

"What time zone are we in?" she asked over the roar of the sea.

"The Awesome Time Zone."

They spent a week living as everyone on Earth should, but only a few are cunning, lucky, or passionate enough to. Moony learned that remembering how to ride a horse is not hard if you're a natural.

When the phone rang for the first time that week, Celia answered it.

"My lady."

"Excuse me? Are you that Russian weirdo?" She looked over at Moony, who was still sleeping. She did not expect to hear the Gypsy's voice on the other end. "Are you in Ecuador?" Celia pictured the figure on the other end of the phone hunched over in a phone booth in the rain.

"I'm around. Look . . ."

Celia actually looked around the room—out the window, a gardener raked sand.

"I appreciate what you're doing."

"What are we doing?"

"Work in the spirit realm. How long will it be before you return?"

"I don't know. Maybe a few more days?"

"Good. I'll arrange the initiation. A little formality I subject all my new acquaintances to."

After hanging up, Celia went into the bathroom to do a few lines. Cocaine in the morning is an irresponsible choice. She realized that later, but not until putting a song on the bedroom sound system: Dillinger's "Cocaine in My Brain." This woke Moony up from a dream where he chased moths at midnight with Kitty, butterfly nets like propellers in the only light source, which revealed itself to be an oncoming train or a snail.

"Huh?"

"Rise and shine, bacon."

"OK."

"Wakey wakey, morning hanky-panky."

"OK."

"Let's do work in the spirit realm."

"Mmm."

"Let's get married."

Moony thought for a moment. Celia danced.

"We should get married." It could work.

"I was just kidding!"

"Oh. I wasn't, so that's a problem." Moony rolled over.

"Now I feel bad, Moony-o."

"Mmm."

"I don't know if I'm ever going to be marriage material."

She ran to the bathroom for a cry and another line.

◆ ◆ ◆

When Celia emerged from the bathroom, her eyes were red, but her pupils were pinpoint sharp.

"I didn't mean to joke about marriage," she said, sitting beside him.

"I didn't mean to not joke about it."

She laughed and then stopped herself because she realized what he said wasn't funny. "You know what's fucked up? I used to think about it. Like, really think about it. Little white dress, little white house, the whole thing. I always dreamed of being the perfect housewife. It's a man's world, so the better I am at being whatever a woman is, I'd have everything taken care of."

"What changed?"

"I met someone." She watched his face. "Before you. A teacher. He made me feel like I had interesting thoughts. Like my opinions about art and life mattered."

Moony wanted to point out to her that what she had described sounded like a predatory relationship dynamic.

"He was married. Is married. But when we'd talk about Diebenkorn or Twombly, I felt like someone worth listening to. Not just"—she gestured at her body—"this."

"You're more than—"

"You don't actually know anything about me." She pulled her knees to her chest.

"I know you. All the details are just information. You're you."

"The teacher—Richard—he thinks I should go to college. Actually learn something instead of pretending all the time."

"Is that what you want?"

"I want to matter for something other than being pretty and available." She touched his hand. "I love you, but you look at me the same way everyone does. Richard looks at me like I could become something."

"So become something."

She shook her head. "I need something that's mine. Tuesdays and Thursdays, I'm going to start taking classes and feel like my brain matters."

"OK," he said.

"OK?" She looked disgusted. "You are so entitled. You can do whatever you want."

"I notice you haven't minded thus far. Here we are in Ecuador, for example."

"Nothing matters to you."

"Take the classes. I want you to be you, even if that means changing."

She kissed him then, and for a moment, it felt like she meant it. But when she pulled away, her eyes were already somewhere else.

❖ ❖ ❖

Driving back to the airport meant an hour-long squint through late-night torrential rain. Moony drove the white rental car down curvy roads much faster than Celia would have approved, but she was sleeping soundly, even making occasional gasps, snorts, and snores anyone in their right mind would find endearing. This triggered in him a change that was not profound. He had decided he would retire from playing video games. Ordinary life could give him thrills if he resolved to spend more time there. What a deal.

The headlights went out, and since there wasn't a city for miles, Moony decided to drive slowly and keep it safe. He discovered that using the hazard lights would provide some illumination both to drive by and to warn oncoming cars. Growing comfortable with this, he sped up to a comfortably unsafe speed and had a good time negotiating how the lights made him dizzy, until he rounded a blind corner and nearly hit an oncoming bicyclist.

What an unlucky rider, he thought to himself and slowed to a stop on the narrow shoulder. *In this rain?*

After opening the driver's side door, Moony cautiously stepped out to wave the bicyclist to his side of the road. Around the corner rumbled a grain truck, which pulverized the front wheel of the bike. The biker tumbled forward and skidded onto the hood of Moony's car. Though the truck veered off the edge of the road to avoid Moony, the trailer it carried jackknifed, dumping hundreds of bushels of wheat over him, the biker, and his car. In the rain, it clung to them as if they had been tarred and feathered.

All was relatively still in the roar of the rain.

To Celia, just waking, it was as beautiful as the Vincent Gallo lyrics she had been humming in her sleep: *I'm always sad, when I'm lonely; I'm always sad, sad . . . It could be so nice, so nice, nice. . .*

The bicyclist on the hood, an older woman, coughed and sat up. Moony was fighting to extricate wheat from his eyes and nose. He thought back to one of the few times his father had taken enough vacation time to go on family trips. They had gone to the Great Sand Dunes.

"The world's biggest sandbox," his father had called it. Moony and Alex buried him up to his face while Joanna watched, peeling her daily grapefruit and casting the peels in front of him. Yvette pretended they had beheaded an evil emperor and danced around him, barefoot on the hot sand.

Celia, in Spanish, asked the bicyclist if she was all right.

"I've seen better days," she responded.

The trucker groaned, trying to free himself from the cab, which rested on its side. "So, America," he said. "What do I owe you for this delight?"

Moony listened as if he didn't speak any other languages. It would have sounded like a man yelling angrily. He tilted his head back to let the rain wash off the rest of the wheat. Scrubbing it out of his hair and off his shoulders, he checked on the biker on his hood. She stretched her legs—everything seemed to be working fine. Not so for her bike. She checked her backpack, which brimmed with small metal canisters, each marked with symbols and alphanumeric labels describing them as rare earth samples. Lithium, cerium, neodymium. The woman was a courier for Adams Minerals. He recognized the alphanumerics on the label.

"Those samples—they're from the Del Norte site?" he asked in English.

The woman's eyes widened slightly, then narrowed. She began to close her backpack.

Moony looked at the courier—really looked at her. Not as an asset or an obstacle, but as a person standing in the rain with a mangled bicycle and a backpack full of mineral samples that might determine the fate of some village he'd never heard of. Her face, angular and weathered from sun. The face of a real person with a real life, probably kids somewhere, maybe a husband who thought she delivered packages for DHL.

The samples in her backpack were the raw materials of someone's future misery. He knew how this worked. His family would outbid the Chinese, secure the rights, bring in the extraction equipment. Within five years, the groundwater would taste like hot garbage. Birth defects would start showing. By decade's end, some nonprofit would publish a report that no one would read about heavy metal poisoning in rural Ecuador.

The woman had her own reasons for being here, her own bills to pay. If he thwarted this woman's courier mission and stopped the deal from happening, it'd be the Chinese running the operation, and that would be even worse.

But then he realized he could make a phone call.

The trucker checked the traffic. It was not clear. Another bicyclist carrying a backpack sped around the corner. The bike slid into the mound of wheat, slowing to a muddy halt. When the traffic was clear, the trucker approached Moony.

Moony spoke. "Let me give you a ride to someplace dry where we can get this matter straightened out."

❖ ❖ ❖

Celia watched an ant carry a peanut shell across the bar's red clay floor.

Moony gave the trucker twice the amount he said he would need.

The biker shot an angry glare at the two men.

Celia gave the woman the remainder of her cocaine. A simple "Gracias" was her reply. Moony wondered how the trip would have been different if he had taken Zelda. Celia and the biker talked for some time while Moony excused himself to make a phone call.

He found a quiet corner near the restrooms and dialed a number. The Ecuadorian Ministry of Environment picked up on the third ring.

"Environmental protection hotline," a woman answered in Spanish.

"I need to report unauthorized mining activity near Del Norte," Moony said, affecting a concerned citizen's tone. "There are foreign companies conducting mineral surveys without proper documentation. They're near protected watersheds."

"Sir, can you be more specific about the location?"

Moony gave her the details he'd seen on the courier's sample containers. "They're collecting lithium samples. I saw them myself —no environmental impact assessments, no community consultations. Just dudes with money."

"And you are?"

"A concerned tourist. I was bird-watching when I saw them." He paused. "They had Chinese equipment, if that matters."

He could hear her typing. Chinese companies were less popular than American ones with the current administration— something about a failed hydroelectric deal.

"We'll send an inspection team," she said. "Thank you for reporting this."

Moony hung up. It wouldn't stop the extraction—nothing could stop the flow of commerce. But it would force his family to file proper paperwork, maybe even implement actual environmental protections. A pain in the ass for sure, but better than letting them run roughshod over another water table.

"It was raining very hard. You must understand I couldn't see you," said the trucker, apologizing as he left.

At the airport, after buying a new suit to replace his wheat-covered clothes, Moony discovered that a message had been left for him: Return to Tulsa instead. Love, The Gypsy.

He considered refusing, telling Celia they should stay in Ecuador where everything felt simpler. Part of him wanted to prove he could be something solid and exciting she could anchor herself to, and maybe that would give her what she needed. She could go to school in Ecuador. Mainly, he just wanted to avoid returning home.

When checking in, he noticed there were two itineraries.

What the hell. He had never been to Tulsa.

❖ ❖ ❖

When they got to Tulsa, his impression was that it was a pint-size hybrid of Dallas and Salt Lake City, and the city would always suck at first glance to those who had seen what the world could really offer, but it would probably turn out to be a nice place.

There was a car for them. Celia got in and drove.

Moony thought about the call he'd made from the bar in Ecuador. Nothing could stop the flow of lithium from ground to battery to smartphone. But Adams Minerals would have to follow protocols now: install water monitoring, compensate local communities. A small wrench in the machine. His father would call it sabotage. But he hadn't blown anything up. He hadn't wanted to. He only wanted to find a less bad outcome.

It had been dumb luck that he'd come into contact with the courier. Like finding a secret level by accident—just random button-mashing. Alex would have immediately called their father, gotten promoted for the intel, and added another line to his résumé. Yvette would have seen the moral implications immediately and acted with conviction. His father would have turned the courier into a true believer before she finished counting her samples. But Moony? Moony had just stumbled into someone else's operation like a drunk wandering into traffic. His brother had inherited the actual business; Moony had inherited the mythology around it.

If he wanted to run anything on his own, he'd need to learn how to make things happen himself.

"You're grinding your teeth," Celia murmured.

"Just thinking about Ecuador."

"The beach was nice."

"Yeah," he said, letting Ecuador sink back into the category of places he'd been once. "The beach was nice."

❖ ❖ ❖

Moony and Celia arrived at the address provided. Moony got out and headed into the theater, humming the underwater theme from *Sonic the Hedgehog*.

Celia had opened her door and was about to follow when someone knocked on her window. A woman with dark hair and an angular face smiled at her.

"You're Moony's girlfriend, right?" Kitty gestured to herself. "Hello Kitty. I know this is strange, but would you like to get coffee while he's in there? These things aren't that interesting to watch."

"But I love art stuff," Celia said, scrunching up her face.

Kitty paused. "Actually, you're already part of it. The whole thing."

"Like in a Marina Abramović piece where the audience doesn't know they're performing, too?"

"What?" Kitty looked embarrassed. "Oh yes, that's right, just like that."

Celia eyed the clouds suspiciously. "Do you think it'll rain later?"

Kitty was already on her way to the passenger door. She opened it and produced a velvet bag of what looked like antique bone dice, the kind that belonged in a museum. "Wanna place wagers?"

Celia shook her head. She didn't gamble.

"Oh, it's not gambling. I wouldn't trust anything to chance. It's all fate. Everything. Sometimes we just need things to represent it for us."

But Celia was already driving, and Kitty had put away the dice.

❖ ❖ ❖

They stood facing a pond across the street from Lazy Susan's Coffee Shop. Celia held a cup of tea and stared at it like it was a bouquet of flowers she didn't know what to do with.

Kitty broke pieces of bread from a roll she'd brought, tossing them toward the water. Celia noticed how the ducks took turns, none pushing too aggressively forward. No fat ducks, no skinny ducks. Just ducks.

"Your boyfriend's family—do you know what they actually do?" Kitty asked carefully.

"Mining company. Minerals. He talks a lot about core samples and cut-off grades and strip ratios sometimes."

"Right. And he's told you about the operations, the assets, all that spy stuff?"

Celia nodded.

"Here's what concerns me," Kitty said, watching the ducks. "He shows up at Sod Hill—clearly placing himself out there, available, like he's looking for work. Takes our money without asking questions. Buys the storage facility without going through proper channels—aggressive, direct. Gets Perry drunk, learns about the surveillance, flips him from informant to ally—all in what, two weeks? When I met him, he dropped some cheesy line that made it sound like he was James Bond. I actually believed him. Even though he acts like an idiot, I want to believe he's part of some shadow organization instead of, you know, bribing senators and underhanded deals, the occasional murder. A company that does regular evil shit."

"But you don't think that anymore."

"My sister does this whole weird thing with everyone she finds interesting. She thinks she's building a network of spiritually activated assets." Kitty tossed bread to the ducks. "But mostly she just . . . opens people up to see what's inside."

"You didn't answer my question. What do you think's inside Moony?"

"I've spent time with him. Enough to know him. The training actually is there—in his body, his instincts, the way he handles situations without thinking. But it's not connected to anything real. He's operating inside this whole buffer of weird imaginary ideas, reacting to some Graham Greene story he's created, but underneath, I keep feeling like I see the real training show through. Which makes him incredibly dangerous because he's looking for some grand purpose rather than confronting the fact that he was raised by run-of-the-mill sociopaths."

"Where did he get this training if you're saying the spy stuff is fake?"

"His whole life was one thing—private schools, martial arts, summer camps, languages. But his insistence that it all meant something specific, that it was preparation for something important—that's the mythology. He read espionage into everything. Turned normal rich kid stuff into operator training. And the weird part is, it could work. If he wanted to, he could make himself into what he imagined he was supposed to be."

Celia watched the ducks. There were two groups—ones that took bread from Kitty and a few farther off in the pond that every few seconds would tilt forward like water-drinking birds, their duck butts to the sky in some form of yogic salute, then bob back up. *Why the two groups?* She wondered about this.

"You're afraid he's playing you."

"I think his unconscious is playing everyone, including him. He was raised by wolves. Now he acts like a sheep, but that won't stop him from moving like a wolf when he needs to."

"So you're saying he's not a spy? He's just so delusional that he's dangerous?"

"I have had the thought that he's some kind of Manchurian candidate."

"I guess that means you both have that very unusual suspicion in common. But why do you care?"

"Because in ten minutes, he could walk out of that theater as someone who actually matters—someone we develop, introduce to our network, put to real use. Or he walks out as another name on a ledger we park money with. Safe and boring." Kitty turned to study Celia's face. "Which would you prefer?"

Celia didn't know how to respond to that. "Let's pretend it's raining," she said suddenly.

"Why?"

"Everything important happens in the rain. In movies, anyway."

Kitty waited for her to give a real answer.

She didn't.

"What if I paid you to leave?" Kitty asked. "Fifty thousand cash. You drive away now, never come back. He'd be taken care of—given purpose, working toward the life he believes he's supposed to have. But you'd be gone."

"Why do I need to be out of the picture for him to have a purpose? Sorry, lady, but who the hell are you to say such a thing? You're just some creep who slept with my boyfriend, and now you want to turn him into a criminal or something. I've been patient with you, but this is beyond fucked up."

"No, no, no, you've got this all wrong. What we do is no more criminal than what your sweet Moon-moon was born into. I think you realize that."

"You're right. Moony *is* sweet."

"We've been watching him for months. The little existence he's built. It's like watching a dog walk in circles before it beds down. But here's what I need to know—are you with him because you love him or because he's rich and aimless enough to let you do whatever you want?"

Celia pressed her heel into the soft bank, feeling the earth grip her shoe as she lifted it. The suction grabbed at her soles with small gasping noises.

"What I think is great about life, a lot of people call ordinary. Sex and just having fun—I don't need my life to be a certain way. The problem with the world, a teacher of mine used to say, is that they mix up ordinary with normal. Normal is the ugliest thing. Neither of us wants to be normal. We want to be ordinary. Art is ordinary. Ordinary is when you don't need to stand out. Normal is when you're afraid to."

"I don't see the difference." *Or the relevance*, Kitty thought.

"Your enemy is Team Normal, too. But you don't want to be ordinary, and we do." Celia stared at the flawless orange of her fingernail polish. She had been complimented more on the striking color of her fingernails than on anything else.

No stranger to redirection, Kitty confided that orange nails reminded her of the cookware her eccentric grandmother used in the 1940s at her Missouri cabin. This led to a twenty-minute conversation on the associations each woman had with Bakelite, eccentric women, and different-colored objects.

Eventually, Kitty realized it was as good an answer as Celia was going to give. "Let's head back," she said. "I'm going to check on him. My sister has plans for him. But I like him. He reminds me of someone who could have been happy if everyone had just left him alone."

"What are you going to do?"

"Tell my sister he's useless. Tell him he passed. Tell you to take him home and keep him there." She paused. "The thing is, he's playing this perfectly–taking our money, not playing into anyone's hand. Even though I don't think he knows he's doing it."

"His unconscious is protecting him."

"I think he really is some kind of self-made sleeper agent, and if we try to make him do what we want, he'll set us all up for a disaster." Kitty studied her. "That means it's best if we distance ourselves, and you keep him happy. Keep him thinking he won by walking away. That's how everyone stays safe–him from us, us from him, and his family from finding out."

"Do you wish you could switch places with me?" Celia said suddenly. "That's not possible, is it?"

Kitty paused. "I believe so."

"Wow. You switch bodies with someone so that you're living their life, and they're living yours?"

From across the pond, an eavesdropping man slapped his forehead.

"I'll go check on him." Kitty said she would see to it that Moony didn't get himself into any trouble if, in exchange, Celia would drive Moony back to Denver as soon as the performance was finished. Before leaving, she ceremoniously tossed a handful of what looked to be bullets into the pond near a placid duck. They slid smoothly into the water without making much of a sound or many ripples.

❖ ❖ ❖

"Take your hat off."

Moony stepped awkwardly over what looked like a hole in the floor. He saw darkness at the bottom. It was a mirror—what he had seen in it was an enormous burned-out bulb on the ceiling thirty feet above him.

The Gypsy's home was an abandoned theater in what seemed to be one of the city's downtowns. Her bedroom and living area filled the stage. It was decorated like a ballroom on the Titanic, a glittering and exhausted 1920s style. Yellowing white drapes remained undusty and continued to impress reflections of tarnished gold woven flowers. The wooden floor, painted black, was replete with trapdoors and chalk outlines of set design memories from at least a decade or two ago. She did not allow hats inside her house. That Moony had made it all the way from the backdoor entrance to center stage still wearing his Denver Broncos cap was a tragedy of possibility for the Gypsy, who attempted tremendous control over her surroundings, both psychic and physical.

Moony obliged, embarrassed at the possibility of having an audience judge him by what he recently discovered was a moderately receding hairline. It was not noticeable, but in a few years, it would be.

Moony stood center stage as the Gypsy applied makeup to his face, her fingers cold and rough.

What a weird place he'd walked right into.

The theater's acoustics were wrong—not just bad, but deliberately disorienting. The way sound bounced created a low-frequency resonance that made his inner ear rebel. It was basically just an old theater, but with a subtle wrongness in proportions that kept the lizard brain on edge. That was because it was a Monarch site, one of those MKUltra offshoots where they'd refined trauma-based conditioning with the aim of creating programmable human assets—individuals who could be triggered to perform specific actions without conscious awareness. The goal was to fragment a subject's identity and rebuild it with controllable components, creating operatives who could be deployed for intelligence operations without remembering their missions afterward. It's well documented that the experiments were massive failures, but the Gypsy felt at home here.

Moony didn't know any of that. But he knew enough was wrong about it to know he wasn't where he wanted to be. His vision started swimming. The makeup she'd applied—of course. She'd dosed him with something. He'd stepped right into the shit again.

Moony's mind drifted to a Halloween when he was ten, and Yvette was twelve. He'd just beaten *Earthworm Jim* and felt unstoppable. They'd decided to go as a two-headed troll, so he'd cut up their father's fishing waders to make the costume.

"I can't believe you just destroyed Dad's Simms," Yvette had said, holding up the severed leg of the waders. "He's going to be furious."

"Boldly going where no troll has gone before," Moony had declared, already wrapping himself in the rubbery material.

They'd won first place at the country club contest. The trophy sat between them in the back seat on the ride home, their mother silent in the front.

Yvette had always liked that about him—his willingness to just do things without overthinking the consequences. But now Moony wondered whether that kind of forward momentum was something best left in childhood. All that remained of that ever-onward clarity was his talent for stumbling into situations without understanding them first.

He discovered to his great disappointment that, in the present moment, he was not with his sister and instead on stage in a theater in Tulsa with a woman who was, he guessed, in the process of putting him through some kind of psychological test. He'd lost touch with the vaguely center-outward awareness that governs the waking mind. He was present but no longer felt housed within himself.

The water-like rustle of a thousand seated theatergoers filled the Gypsy's home. She stood center stage making conversation with Moony about something he couldn't bear to have interest in. He thought he saw Heath sitting in the front row, petting his sleeping puppy, his own ears roving through the sea of audience chatter like those of a nervous animal searching for its owner. The Gypsy was opening and closing her mouth, and when she did so, words and sounds came out in staccato lines toward the far end of the audience. There was no curtain—she was announcing a performance center stage while the audience watched and conceptualized their response to what some suspected were arbitrary acts. These people believed that life was meaningless in a bad way, and they enjoyed seeing it staged.

Moony's mind became one with Heath, who might or might not have been present in the theater. Every theater performance always had something to do with the audience's internal response, Heath felt. The world, upon viewing, fictionalized. He could smell it. It smelled like a Halloween mask to him.

The Gypsy stood before him in red silk, sprouting her word salad: "Houses are amphitheaters of thought. Horses are tight ambulances . . ."

The words started to take on color and multiply. He could visually analyze the linguistic patterns with his waking eyes–semantic satiation through repetition–but knowing the mechanism didn't stop it from working. His brain was trying to make meaning from meaninglessness, and whatever she'd dosed him with made every connection feel painfully profound.

"Stop," Moony said, sitting down on the stage floor. The word came out wrong, like "Soup," and he wondered if he'd actually said it or just thought it.

In the audience, three figures swam in and out of focus: Kitty in the front row (or was it three Kittys?), a muscular man who looked like trouble (his face kept shifting into Moony's father's), and someone in a hoodie (Yvette? No, stop that, she's dead).

He needed an anchor. The money. He began miming counting bills. The physical motion helped, gave his fracturing perception something to organize around.

"One thousand, two thousand, three thousand . . ."

Was this what Yvette had felt? This dissociation, this sense of watching yourself from outside? "I've seen how the sausage gets made," she'd said.

The real joke was that nobody's irreplaceable. Not the gardener, not the loved one, not even the guy who signs the checks. Moony's father ran operations on three continents, but he was so effective at getting everyone to fear him that not a single person actually liked him. Moony wondered if anyone would notice if he disappeared tomorrow.

"You must shoot," the Gypsy insisted, pressing a gun into his hand. "Choose your target."

The weight of the gun, a CZ-75 PCR, led him to believe its fifteen-round magazine was loaded. But surely it hadn't been filled with live rounds. Although even blanks could be dangerous. *Has anyone here signed a liability waiver?* he wondered. *Is there anyone else physically present besides me?* He had three options—no, infinite options—no, three:

Option one: Play along. Shoot something symbolic. Give them the psychodrama they want. Let them think they'd cracked him open and found something useful inside. Go back to Denver and proceed to follow whatever orders come his way and, in all ways, become Dan Adams's wayward son.

Option two: Flip the script. Turn predator. These people were amateurs playing with tools they didn't understand. He could destroy them without firing a shot. All it would take was a few phone calls to the right people. Or, even better, find ways of enlisting them and claiming control of their network. His father might even be proud—finally showing initiative, finally playing the game.

Option three: Something stupid. Something that wasn't from his training or his rebellion against it. Something actually his.

"Fort thousand, five prowsand . . ." He kept counting, his face numb, speaking louder now. The repetition was helping, and it was also buying time. Time to figure out what the fuck he actually wanted.

The Gypsy's words washed over him. "How you confront the demon makes that demon what it is."

"Tunny tousand, twenty-one thousand . . ."

He thought of Perry. There was something genuine about Perry's enthusiasm for his half-baked schemes that Moony envied. The man threw himself into each new venture—movie screenings, cappuccino bar upgrades, mobile tool rental, community art shows—with the desperate conviction of someone who believed that the next project might finally be the one that transformed him into something more than a sexually confused ex-cop property manager in a golf-themed apartment complex. Perry wasn't playing at being ordinary the way Moony was; he was ordinary, showing it to the world with every fiber of his being. Perhaps that's why Moony felt so comfortable around him —they were opposites striving for the same middle ground.

What did Moony want? The question felt like looking into the sun, except the sun was wearing his face and counting money.

"Fifty thousand, sippy-cup thousand . . ."

The stage lights started to strobe. Multiple Gypsies stood before him now, all holding guns, all demanding he choose. His fractured vision showed him every possible version of this moment:

- The version where he shot himself and they all applauded his commitment.
- The version where he shot the Gypsy and took over her operation.
- The version where the Gypsy shot him and walked away counting money.

- The version where he was still in Denver, playing video games with Celia next to him, and none of this was happening. He liked that version very much.

"You thought you were testing me," he heard himself say, though he wasn't sure if he was speaking to the Gypsy or himself. "But this was my test for you."

The words felt true and false. Everything was a test for everyone. That was the problem.

That was why Yvette had done it.

She'd left everyone. Joanne, Alex, him. Chosen death over compromise. But she'd also left a hole that pulled at everyone around it. Moony thought of Perry waiting for him back in Denver, probably planning another venture. Deb inviting more romance. Heath in communion with inanimate objects. That was his team. Those were his fellow operatives. Yvette had left. He wouldn't.

Don't lose count.

"Hunner thousand, hunner and one sand . . ."

He stood up, the movement making the room spin along all three axes: X, Y, and Z. The Gypsy looked worried now. Or was that just what he wanted to see?

"I always thought psyops was a lot like aromatherapy," he said, and it didn't make sense, so it was true, but saying it felt like admitting defeat. Like being exactly what they'd made him to be.

"Two hundred thousand . . ."

He dropped the magazine from the gun and cycled the slide to eject what looked and felt like a perfectly functional nine millimeter bullet into his palm. He wondered how he'd been stacking money while he'd held a gun in his hand. He counted his hands. He looked for the money.

"Two hundred fifty thousand. That's what you left at my apartment. And MILF invested it."

Her face was a spiraling vortex.

"I'm already activated," Moony said, or thought he said. "Sod Hill. Deep cover. You're not cleared." The Gypsy's face shifted. Was she disappointed?

He walked off stage, repeating the phrase "all for just a quarter mill" over and over again to maintain what was left of his cognitive function.

And then he hadn't walked off stage, but time had passed. He felt sober and was holding a cup of tea.

◆ ◆ ◆

Thirteen Moonies sat in a semicircle holding cups of tea. He'd become every figure at the table in *The Last Supper*.

He had a splitting headache.

Theater, Moony thought, *was stupid*.

He could feel the weight of the gun and the magazine in his pocket. He looked down and wondered why his suit was soaked with sweat.

"You're doing fine," Kitty said, appearing with a dustpan full of dead moths. In this light, she looked less like the Gypsy's sister and more like her younger self.

The Gypsy stood ten feet away, arms crossed, watching him with the patience of someone who'd done everything before. Her face was lined in a way Moony hadn't noticed earlier. She looked like a tired human. But the way the theater's bad lighting caught her, she could have been standing in a doorway to somewhere else entirely. He couldn't be sure she herself wasn't a portal to another realm.

"The email you sent—the one from my family's domain, pretending to be about Jon-Jon," Moony said, his voice raw. "Why did you do that?"

"You bought the property without following any protocol. I needed more material on you to see how you'd react."

"You got me drugged."

The Gypsy waved this away like he'd complained about the temperature. "These things help reveal what's happening one or two layers deeper in the psyche."

Moony looked up at the rigging above the stage—pulleys, ropes, the manipulative bones of theater.

"You said something earlier," the Gypsy said, "about being activated. About deep cover."

Moony's mouth was dry. "Did I?"

"Don't play games like I can't see all sides of you. With the rental property, you leaped in with both feet. You saw an opportunity and took it."

"That was dumb of me."

"That was instinct." She moved closer. "That's what I've been waiting for."

Moony, for some reason, thought of his father, and all he could see or feel was a black hole.

"The property was just the beginning. Now we talk about real work."

"I already have work."

Agitated silence. Both sisters studied him. The Gypsy looked ready to walk away. Then Kitty spoke: "Whiskey Ringo Kawabata."

Moony blinked. "What?"

"November sparrow in the half dawn."

He stared at her. "Are you having a stroke?"

She said phrases in Russian. Strings of numbers, maybe geographic coordinates. Names of places from his childhood. Moony's mind wandered to *Metal Gear Solid*. There was this moment in the game when Snake realizes he's been fed false memories, that his entire identity might be fabricated.

"Someone really locked you down. I've studied all the techniques, and I can't seem to find the right activation sequence for you." The Gypsy's eyes narrowed. "You're a gun without a trigger."

He thought of the life awaiting him back at Sod Hill. Yvette had chosen to leave—leave the family, leave the whole game, leave life itself—rather than stay complicit. He understood that choice. She'd seen what staying meant and refused it. But someone had to remain. Someone had to hold position. That was his mission now—maintaining presence in a location anyone of interest would consider beneath notice. Deep cover meant accepting assignments that looked like failure. Perry, Deb, Heath, Celia—they were his responsibility now. People to protect by staying close. Sod Hill was strategic positioning.

"You wouldn't understand the level I'm operating at."

"Moony—"

"Whiskey Kawasaki motorboat," Moony said suddenly, throwing her own tactic back at her. "You'd better watch out, or I might do something to burn your operation."

She smiled. "What?"

"November. Sparrow at the threshold. Is that how this works? You say the words; I activate?" He laughed, and it sounded unhinged. "But I'm already activated. I've been activated since I moved to Sod Hill."

She stared at him. The theater's strange acoustics made the silence sound like whispers.

"I've heard enough from you for all time," the Gypsy said flatly. "We'll have our tenants, inflated rates, cash deposits—you'll deposit the checks, pay your taxes, provide the paper trail. You're our shell company. That's all."

"That's better than I deserve."

"Yes." The Gypsy stepped close. "But you're no risk to us." She stopped and looked at Kitty. "You really need to be more discerning."

Kitty didn't take any offense. "He's not like us. He doesn't want to be"

The Gypsy studied him for a long moment. "Goodbye, Moony," she said finally. "You're more like your father than you know."

"Nobody's perfect," Moony said. "But he wants to run the world. I'm on a mission to fuck my girlfriend and landlord and drink beer with my . . . other landlord."

"Such modest ambitions."

"The best kind."

"Don't think I'm threatened by any of this. You can't burn what's unburnable. Our reports go through three handlers before they reach anyone real. It's shells all the way down, жучок." The Russian endearment—little bug—made him realize she'd been speaking Russian this whole time. Or had she? When had he learned Russian? His father had insisted on—

He was already on his way off stage toward the exit door. He wasn't sure if he hated artists or if he wished he could become one. Had this been a performance, or was the rest of the world also as hollow as this felt?

As he left, he heard Kitty say something about second chances and how this was all a part of a larger spiritual process, but he was already gone.

Moony got in the car and said hello to the three Celias at the steering wheel. They each raised an eyebrow at him. He slumped in the passenger seat. "Let's go."

As they pulled away, Moony wondered if this was what freedom felt like. He didn't know if he'd won or lost. He knew he would always refuse to play the game.

❖ ❖ ❖

The air vent on the rented Ford kept wolf whistling.

"Oh, it does that," Celia said, driving her way out of Tulsa on a suddenly windy and rainy April day, pursing her lips and blowing a kiss at the vent to tease an admiring stranger.

The sun was nowhere to be found, tucked behind clouds and the few tall buildings in the area. She was wondering what turn of events could have led her to a duck pond in Oklahoma near a theater where her boyfriend played with a gun on stage.

❖ ❖ ❖

Out the window of the rented Ford, a man held up a cardboard sign with the peace symbol, nothing else. It was soggy from the rain. The man, wearing a poncho, seemed content. He gave a thumbs-up to the passing Ford. Moony wondered at the man's existence, and as he wondered, his gawk became more dignified, slightly stoic.

Celia, fantasizing about being a robot with the world's smoothest joints, dripping with oil, pulled up to the pump at Quik Trip. Celia had this fantasy every so often. She didn't know why. Neither do you.

Moony hopped out to pump the gas.

The man with the cardboard sign approached. He said. "I'm with the API, the Association for Poor Indians. If you have any donations, they'd really help us out." He extended a Styrofoam cup.

Moony looked down and pulled four hundred dollars from his wallet. The man took it nonchalantly.

"Thanks. Could I get a cigarette–does your lady friend have a cigarette?"

Celia stepped out of the car, heading toward the Quik Trip.

"Ma'am, you have a smoke? I'm with the Native American Peace Alliance, and every cigarette counts."

She shook her head and looked down, adjusting her jacket tighter.

"You two have a lovely day." He walked away into the rain without an umbrella.

Moony thought about what he and the API/NAPA man had in common. He thought about what they did not have in common. The pump clicked off at a price of exactly fifty dollars. Moony pressed the button that declared no, he did not wish to have his car washed today, then jogged inside. His suit shed water marvelously. The gun felt heavy in his pocket, and it looked very much like a gun, but since he did not want to draw attention to himself by feeling uncomfortable, he pretended he was carrying several rolls of quarters and walked naturally, as if into an arcade.

He loved the consumer smell of convenience stores more than most people seemed to fantasize about the smell of rain. Taking a leak, he thought about how nice it would be to get a yacht. Maybe he and Celia could sail to someplace trashy. The bathroom was out of paper towels, so he didn't wash his hands. He purchased some beef jerky on the way out of the store, making an extra effort to be kind to the cashier, whose name was Ted. Ted was overweight in a way that had given him considerable breasts, Moony noticed.

Outside, the world felt hollowed out. Rain fell in vertical lines, making the same sound on every surface. The parking lot was empty except for their Ford and a truck idling somewhere out of sight. Moony walked to the car and noticed a spot on his face that was still tacky where the Gypsy had applied makeup. He touched his jaw and felt the residue—waxy, slightly gritty. Like wearing someone else's skin.

"You mind if I drive?" Moony asked.

"Be my guest," she answered.

Moony thought about growing a big beard, a full beard. He could do it, if he could make it through the difficult itchy period of stubble. Celia might mind. Maybe he would be away for several days, and he could surprise her with a beard. Moony with a beard. He hoped she wasn't sleeping with someone else anymore.

She reclined her seat after giving him directions to the interstate.

A commercial came on the radio—something about home security systems. "Protect what matters most," the voice said. Moony thought of Sod Hill. Perry, Deb, Heath, Celia. His team. His mission. Best decision he'd ever made.

Celia contented herself to lie in peace and silence as he drove.

Moony turned down the radio's volume and was attentive to the sounds of her sleep. The clock on the stereo read 2:20 p.m. He had been awake all night, but more than anything, he did not want to lose this day to drowsiness. Things had happened he felt would drift away unless he took them into himself, deep in his psyche.

Already he was forgetting the activation phrases the Gypsy had tried. Whiskey something. November. One had sounded like a name—Kawasaki, maybe. *I should write them down*, he thought. Then: *Why?* If they did work, writing them down was dangerous. He left them to fade. He was already deep in his real assignment now anyway.

His hands felt strange on the steering wheel—too light, too certain. Like they knew where to be without him deciding. Had he always moved this way and just never noticed? He flexed his fingers, watching them.

The real activation code had probably come during *Double Dragon*. Some combination of button presses he'd executed thousands of times until his muscle memory made it automatic. Or was it that thing Celia did with her hips?

He made it to some town in Kansas he figured was halfway to Denver from Tulsa. When he pulled into another gas station to tell her he'd like to switch, she kissed his cheek and proposed that they just get a hotel since there was no rush. He said he'd rather get back, if she felt comfortable enough to drive.

She asked, "Are you sure?" and Moony nodded.

Moony fell asleep and had terrible dreams.

He was haunted by one in particular, where there was a heavy iron chain, green with moss, extending deep into a warm lake. In the dream, he was a camera following the chain down to the bottom. It was dark, but he could see that it was fastened into the Earth somehow. Down at the lake's bottom, he was intrigued by the multicolored soil and became aware that the water level was rising.

After waking, he wondered what the dream might mean.

Celia's idea was that it was "weird," the same idea Moony had about it.

It was morning when they got back to Sod Hill. Perry was in the yard picking up trash around the mailboxes. He smiled and waved.

He looks good doing what he does, Moony thought and waved back.

❖ ❖ ❖

In an hour, the satanist knocked on Moony's door.

Since it was before ten-thirty in the morning, it took several rounds of knocking. Moony opened the door, audibly scratching his balls. Yawning, he asked "What?" and tried to be polite.

"Here's the thing. See, normally I'm the one cleans the pool, but not anymore. I've been demoted since I suck at it, Deb says you do yard work now and get free rent."

"What's that on your neck?"

Josh touched the nine-pointed star hanging from a leather cord. "I'm Baha'i now."

"What happened to the prince of darkness?"

"Satan was a phase. This is about unity. The oneness of humanity." He said it the way he used to say, "Hail thyself."

"Huh."

"Best decision I ever made."

Moony closed his door and fell asleep face down on his couch.

❖ ❖ ❖

Moony tromped into the Sod Hill office with a couple of folders full of incorporation documents. Perry was inside reading a Louis L'Amour paperback, sitting in a reclining padded metal office chair that squeaked like a haunted playground anytime he did so much as turn the page.

"MILF is now officially a property management company," he said to Perry, sliding papers across the desk. "We handle maintenance, tenant relations, and rent collection for Aurora AAAA Storage."

Perry squinted at the paperwork. "Since when do you know about property management?" His breath smelled like an Egg McMuffin.

"Since I hired a company that does. They take fifteen percent, handle everything. I just own it." Moony pulled out his phone, showing Perry the month's deposits. "Seventeen thousand after expenses. Clean money from regular tenants paying regular rent."

"What about those special units? One-forty-seven through one-fifty-three?"

"What special units?" Moony set his face like Christopher Walken delivering a monologue about nothing in particular—eerily calm with just enough pause between blinks to make everyone uncomfortable. "According to our records, those are long-term tenants with standard contracts. They pay a high rate because they're climate-controlled units."

"By my reckoning, I guess that means you don't have to worry about the Gypsy or anyone hanging anything over your head, liability-wise. But she fronted you the money; doesn't she expect you to pay her?"

"She got exactly what she paid for—a clean property deed in someone else's name that she can rely on just like any other paying customer."

"That the sort of stuff you learned from your dad?"

"More like from video games." Moony shook his head. "In Super Mario, you can skip entire worlds if you know where the warp pipes are hidden. Turns out money laundering works the same way."

❖ ❖ ❖

His second day on the job, Moony worked cleaning trash around the dumpsters, then the mailboxes, when he came across an advertisement for a new kind of construction in which a giant 3-D printer machine pooped out concrete in slow layers until it made an entire house. He wondered what the big deal was about that, why that was supposed to be better than just having people stack bricks to build a house.

"Hey," said someone in a smoky monotone voice from the window of a slowly passing Cadillac. It was his brother Alex, probably late on his way to someplace crummy. Two pretty girls sat in the back seat together.

Moony looked down at his clothes—he wore cheap blue jeans and a Broncos jersey. He wasn't wearing shoes. His toenails were untrimmed. There was dirt underneath them.

"For a second there, I thought you were the gardener. You got a tan, bro." He winked, which could have meant many things.

A dog whined and whined in the distance.

Alex winked again.

"You mind filling me in on what you're doing here?" Moony said.

"Hop in."

He did.

"I'm Taylor."

"Hi, I'm Ingrid."

"Nice to meet you both."

Moony and Ingrid used to be friends when they were both very young–they played hide and seek–but neither remembered the other now.

The white Cadillac, the parking lot.

"Dan Senior kicked the bucket. Time for me to step up."

Ingrid and Taylor had apparently not heard the news.

"Funeral's in an hour."

"You're a cold one," Moony said. Only now that it was too late did he wish he'd said goodbye. Or maybe just said something real to the old man, once. A strange gratitude rose in him–for the training, the money, even the neglect that had taught him to disappear into video games and find his own peace. Gratitude, too, that he'd never have to see him again, never have to wonder if this would be the day Dan Senior finally decided his son was good enough.

"He's dead now. I'll give you a ride."

"I can't go wearing this."

"Meet you there, then." Alex would grow up to be just like Dan Senior. He pulled into a handicapped parking space to let out Moony, who walked into the Sod Hill office.

Deb was chewing on the end of a number-two pencil when Moony walked into her office. On her desk was a stack of flyers that read:

Residents,

After a lot of detective work, the hidden camera pervert has been caught. The bathroom in the gym is secure again. Many apologies for this intrusion into your privacy. The employee responsible has been dealt with.

Management

The man who looked like God had been right. It was Julio.

He kissed her neck just once. She had gotten a new haircut. He said it looked nice and that he'd have to take the rest of the day off for a funeral. Out the window behind her, Moony saw his brother run past, carrying a trash can above his head.

Deb placed her hand on Moony's, looking in his eyes.

There was a loud crash outside. It sounded a lot like a garbage can smashing into some mailboxes, then into some bushes.

"I'll secure the perimeter." Moony felt good saying that. He hadn't felt good in a while. He kissed her again and left.

Alex kicked over a recycling bin, sending bottles rolling across the artificial turf. "Look at this shithole. Probably killed the old man, knowing you ended up here. Plastic grass? Jesus." He picked up another rock, hurled it at a decorative lamp post. "You're cleaning toilets for losers while the family business—"

The rock bounced off the post and struck someone's windshield. A spider web of cracks spread across the glass.

"—goes to people who actually give a damn about heritage."

Moony felt a circuit breaker flip inside him. He stepped forward and caught Alex with a clean right cross, positioning his weight so his brother's momentum carried him backward. Alex's feet tangled on the curb, and he went down hard on the artificial turf, his midback landing on one of his thrown rocks. It knocked the breath out of him, but the bastard had too much pride to let it show.

"The funeral's in Boulder, not Denver, like Dad wanted it to be," Alex said.

❖ ❖ ❖

"Well, you do look like a goddamned gardener," Joanna said. She wiped her eyes with a Kleenex, though she hadn't been weeping. She was one to reserve drama for less obvious times.

She made a face at him, rolling her eyes. "You could at least stop picking at the hedges. Either get some shears and a salary or put your paws in your pockets."

They were outside on a warm, still day on top of a gentle hill in Boulder Cemetery. Beneath puffy white clouds, Dan Senior's headstone was seven feet, eight inches tall—enough, but not too much, everyone felt.

"What did he die of?" asked someone.

Nibbling her pinkie nail, Moony's mother replied, "His heart wasn't ever that good." Her eyes were beautiful and bored.

Moony had given his brother a black eye. Joanna winked at it.

"Will she remarry?" someone asked.

Across the cemetery, Moony spotted Zelda in a black dress that he remembered her not wearing. She stood next to a guy in an ill-fitting suit who kept checking his phone. The man had one of those hypermasculine-style beards that was trimmed to make it look like he had a sharper jawline. Moony remembered how she'd arched her back when she came. Now she was here with this mouth breather who probably talked about cryptocurrency at parties.

Their eyes met. She gave him a therapist's smile. She walked over, leaving the guy squinting at his phone.

"I'm sorry for your loss," she said, using her counseling voice.

"Thanks. You here for someone?"

"My boyfriend went to school with your brother. Chad wanted to pay respects."

Chad. Of course.

"That's him?" Moony glanced at the guy now taking a selfie with the cemetery in the background.

"He has an original take on mortality," she said, like she was diagnosing someone not present. "Death makes him need to document his aliveness."

"And you're into that?"

She studied him. "Sometimes what's best isn't what's best. You know?"

Chad wandered over, hand extended. "You must be the brother. Sorry for your loss, bro. Your dad was a real titan."

"A real one," Moony said.

"Cool, cool. I'm in app development. Disrupting the funeral industry, actually." Chad laughed at his own observation.

Zelda touched Chad's arm. "We should let him get back to his family."

As they walked away, Moony heard Chad asking if she thought the cemetery had good Wi-Fi. If she was choosing that, what did it mean that she'd chosen him?

Moony brought Ingrid and Taylor to his mother, introducing them as his friends. He hoped the three would talk with each other, but they had almost no common ground and very little interest.

He asked if he could get them anything to drink.

"I'm seventeen," Ingrid said. "Bottled water."

Taylor was fine and didn't need anything.

Joanna told Ingrid that it was before noon anyway, and no one but a lush had alcohol in the morning, least of all at a public gathering. She ordered Perrier.

At the grave, Moony stood between his mother and a cousin he didn't recognize. Alex gave the eulogy—smooth, practiced, exactly the right number of words like *courage* and *commitment to excellence*.

"Our father taught us that opportunity favors the prepared," Alex said. "He prepared us all for different roles."

Moony thought about those roles. Yvette had been prepared to run the Montana operation, and she chose not to become that person. Alex, the youngest, had been prepared to follow in his father's footsteps with a complete lack of irony or self-awareness. And Moony—what had he been prepared for?

His father had once called him "the enthusiastic one," which, at the time, Moony had taken as praise. No one before or since would describe Moony as enthusiastic. But watching Alex work the crowd after the service, he understood what it probably meant: Moony was the one who wanted to believe in something, and belief was not a job qualification.

Yvette had seen clearly and checked out. Alex had seen clearly and played the game anyway. Moony had invented a game nobody else was playing and been confused when some Romanian weirdo suddenly passed him the ball.

What remained of the burial of Dan Senior, who was a rich and powerful man, was a dull event.

* * *

The first call to the family accountant was the hardest.

"Mr. Adams, I'm not sure I understand. You want to redirect your distributions?"

"The Sod Hill Arts Guild. I've set that up. And I want my share of the estate converted to a trust that I can't draw from personally."

"Sir, that's several million dollars annually."

"I'm very aware."

"And you want to live on … your property management income?"

"It's more than most get by on."

The accountant was quiet for a long moment. "Your brother won't like this."

"Alex is about to have a much more complicated life." Moony smiled at the ceiling. "When the distributions stop coming to me, they'll have to be reaccounted for somewhere. And I want to make sure they go through channels that require actual documentation. Legal documentation. The kind that gets audited."

"Mr. Adams–"

"I'm going to make it very hard for Adams Minerals to do anything that isn't perfectly legitimate. That's part of the operation."

After he hung up, he felt the simple satisfaction of making someone's life more difficult through perfectly legal means.

This, it turned out, was something he was actually trained for.

❖ ❖ ❖

Frog House had never looked so artsy: sleek televisions with imitation gold leaf affixed to their borders had entirely replaced the older rear-projection models, the floor had been polished to highlight the brass frogs set into the tile, green marble baseboards were installed around the perimeter, and the wet bar itself was replaced by an artisan model produced in near-exact imitation of the truly wonderful Bar il Palio in Siena, Italy.

Moony, hair longer and slicked back like a greaser, wearing a blue work shirt and corduroy pants, pressed a button underneath the main bar, and the new German vinyl shutters swung open, allowing in the eleven o'clock alpine light. He squinted his eyes against it.

The telephone rang, so he walked outside. The air smelled of hay at first, then of cattle, then of cow shit. The odor lingered as Moony watered the ornamentals around the entryway.

The spring air was crisp and perfect, the temperature ideal.

A Lincoln Town Car pulled up. A skinny man rolled down the window. "Is this the venue where they do the art film screenings?"

"Positively is. Today we're showing both the old and the new *Planet of the Apes*, pretty much back to back."

"Oh wow, I still haven't seen the new one. Tim Burton, right?"

"Are you a fan?"

"I couldn't get enough of *Edward Scissorhands*."

"That was Johnny Depp."

The driver paused, guessing that Moony was uninformed. "Yeah. So I guess I'm a little early."

"Come on in."

"Can I park here?"

"If you're handicapped."

"I'm a marathon runner."

"Then you'll have to park on the street."

Moony walked inside, hand on his budding gut. It takes effort to let oneself go, and he was ready to start, with the work ethic of a person floating downstream for as long as possible. His and Celia's relationship had been succeeding, he believed, largely a result of their willingness to accept each other's flaws, even be attracted to them. Celia was happy because she knew Moony did not ask her to be faithful, and yet she was faithful. She pursued her education and wherever it might lead. The distance between them was ideal, though compromised; the tension in their relationship was necessary, as if it were an entity they both required—a quiet yet powerful third person in the couple who held equal status with both of them. They were very much in love with this shadow person.

Moony was alone in the bar. Perry had passed on to him managerial duties for both lawn care and the art movie screenings at Frog House after only a week of being continually impressed with his abilities and gave him a small hourly wage in addition to free rent. So far, with the income from his storage unit business, he had bought a new vehicle: a plain white van, the interior of which he had gutted and was gradually converting into a bona fide glamping vehicle.

The arrival of this object caused Heath to deduce that he was being spied on—a white van parked conspicuously below his apartment, day and night. He was certain he had seen these things happen before and knew they must point to a future that saw him moving out. He'd retired from the manufacture and use of meth, even though selling was easy—the location was central to the large number of South Englewood buyers. He needed a fresh start since he no longer saw the face of God in his stainless steel pot, which was because he had begun taking the antipsychotic drug Aripiprazole, which gave him insomnia but allowed him back onto the brain's familiar iceberg's tip of thinking—he could not sleep but was able to socialize at late hours with strangers without giving them much of an impression that he was cognitively unstable.

He met a few girls, and he fell in love with one named Quinn, who was more patient and polite than any woman he had before dreamed of and altogether without ulterior motives; he felt she was perfect. He wanted to move in with her, and she had not objected to this. Though she disapproved of his meth habit, she did not despise him for it or discourage him from manufacturing it.

As it went, Quinn worked in a rehabilitation clinic; not surprisingly, she was a former addict. She was short, her hair was black and straight, and she always wore jeans except when swimming, which wasn't often. She had slept with twenty-one men and two women before meeting Heath. She had been in love three times before she and Heath fell in love. They kept no secrets from each other. Their affection was raw and unadorned. Many therapists would object to their codependence and enmeshment, but it worked well for them.

Moony was there the morning Heath moved out, and he had helped him box up some of his things: in the front room, lots of fire extinguishers, pots, chemicals, containers. In the bedroom, vintage baseball posters, lawn furniture, an air mattress, religious texts. Moony tried but could not make an articulate judgment on the character of these possessions. When he told Heath goodbye, he meant well. They both felt like real human beings thankful they had nowhere impressive to escape to.

When Heath entered Frog House, he looked around, taking in the scene. "You really did a number–a number one on this place." Moony associated the phrase *number one* with urination, so it took him a moment to realize Heath was not inferring that he had pissed on the bar.

Quinn entered also, carrying a decidedly obsolete VHS camcorder. Moony realized at once the truth that she and Heath were meant for each other. All the same, when they kissed, he became a little sad.

The marathon runner and several slight women entered, followed by a crowd of regulars: Celia, Josh the Baha'i guy, Perry, Deb, and the others. The drug addicts, role-playing gamers, sex offenders, and magicians had all been kicked out for one thing or another.

When it was time, Moony started the screening and sat down in what had become his usual chair. He had scrawled "Moony's ass here" on the seat of it. The old *Planet of the Apes* bore some substance, but the remake did not. Perry found it likable but admitted to the discussion circle that it was not as great as the first.

When the screenings concluded, Moony got behind the bar and made drinks. True to form and happy to be assigned a role, he did an excellent job and made himself forgettable. When his brother entered the bar, Moony did not lose momentum, asking "What can I get for you, brother?"

Alex looked like their father's sequel—everything Dan Senior wanted in a son carved into flesh. Sharp suit, jaw set like he was permanently disapproving of something. He moved through the bar like he was doing it a favor.

Josh swiveled around on his barstool and extended to Alex his black-fingernailed hand. "Hello."

Alex, still watching Moony, asked "What is this, your new family of rednecks?"

Josh withdrew his handshake and glared at him. His eyes found Alex's Ozzy Osborne key ring, which Alex laid on the bar.

"How's the South American paperwork going?" asked Moony, polishing the inside of a beer mug with his apron.

Alex sat down next to Josh, not noticing how vengefully he was being regarded. Moony, entertained, shook his brother a martini.

"I remember when we were little, you seemed like James Bond to me. Now you seem more like, I don't know, a retired tennis coach."

Moony laughed. "I drive Bond's car, at least."

"Double-oh seven drove a goddamn Aston Martin. Not a van."

"So do thousands of people."

Alex sipped his drink. "I hate martinis. But this one's pretty good."

Julio, appearing from the bathroom, asked if anyone had heard his story about horse racing. No one said they hadn't, and he left through the back door.

Moony set down the polished martini shaker and asked Alex, "So who died? Did you die, or did someone crawl up your ass and die?"

Alex ran his hand through his hair and gulped down the rest of his martini. Looking macho despite stifling a retch, he said, "Don't count on it." The expression on his face didn't look like a smile, but it may have been. It was difficult to tell. He looked like such a tough guy.

With Deb standing by looking as if she wanted to give Alex a hug, he decided that he had better be going. Moony asked if he had just stopped by to get a free drink and some attention from Deb.

Alex looked at Deb and laughed. Deb laughed back, more in his face than he thought possible. The aggression of a compassionate person can be truly terrifying.

Josh took the opportunity to steal Alex's house key off his key ring. He later offered it to Deb as a gift. She declined but tousled her blonde hair and smiled sweetly at him.

Moony watched his brother take out a ten, lay it on the bar, snatch up his keys, and walk out. Not caring to say anything to Alex, he put the ten in the cash drawer.

"You know what I love?" Heath screamed happily, running toward the door, arms linked with Quinn's. "I love ass!"

On their way out, they tromped into Alex so clumsily it must have been choreographed.

It gave Alex a black eye.

* * *

In Sod Hill's main office lounge, Deb ate cotton candy while Moony and Perry spoke of their big plans.

"As the operations develop, they'll start to pay for themselves," Moony assured him.

They were generating ideas for the next art show. So far, they hadn't been able to get any sort of deal with the Denver Art Museum, but they would continue to try.

"It's like we get to be talent scouts for local artists," Moony said.

Perry agreed. "Pretty soon, we'll make a name for Sod Hill. I'm thinking we could get nothing but artists, musicians, and those types living here. Whenever the leases expire on the turds occupying our domiciles presently, we'll make a move to inject some creative people into this complex."

"Please don't call them domiciles," Deb said. Her lips were stained pink from the cotton candy. "Anyway, the worst occupants are gone already. Out with turds, in with talent." She extended her arms like a proud belly dancer.

"We could give coupons for rent deductions based on each tenant's creativity," said Moony.

"Not a bad idea," Perry said, writing it down.

"What about a Halloween party?" asked Deb. "Costume design is art."

"We could do our own exhibit," Moony proposed.

"The one we keep talking about—a series of photographs of people taking public transportation and brief bios and interviews with the people," said Perry.

"We could call it 'Who's Taking the Bus?'" Moony said.

Deb stood up and clapped her hands, excited. "We could do sketches for some, maybe, instead of photos."

"I can't draw," Perry confessed.

Moony couldn't, either.

"We could still draw something and say middle school kids did them," Perry said.

"Or asylum people, for my drawings." Moony fumbled with his pencil. "I would need to practice, even for that."

Deb took off her dress, her bra, her panties, but left on her leggings and heels. "Draw me."

Moony got up and locked the door.

For half an hour, Deb reclined in the chair, legs crossed. She held a pencil like a cigarette and rested her head on her wrist, looking pensive.

The drawings turned out terribly.

Moony's was grossly disproportionate (Deb called it a fertility figure), and Perry had drawn faintly, clearly paying too much attention to her face, especially her eyes, to do any justice to her figure.

They compared drawings, and each said, "Not bad" at the same time.

❖ ❖ ❖

Celia looked at her face in the mirror, waiting for the toilet to finish flushing before opening the bathroom door.

"Baby." She called for Moony.

"Sweetie?" He approached, beer in hand. He watched himself grow larger in the bathroom mirror as he got nearer.

Celia put out her hand. Like a movie so trite neither of them could watch without feeling dirty, he took her hand and spun her.

He ignored knocking his elbow on the wall.

They kissed.

Out of her half-closed eyelids, she looked at a photo on the wall she had not noticed before. In it, Kitty wore a wide-brimmed straw hat and an Old West–style dress. It was taken at a carnival, though it was weathered to look antique. She leaned on a horse-hitching post, squinting at the camera as if it were difficult to read.

Celia motioned to the photograph. "Is this new?"

"She sent a big one to Perry and Mom as an early wedding present. She said it was good luck that I had one, too."

"I love you," she whispered into his ear. She meant it.

"We're perfect for each other," he echoed.

He ran his fingers through her fingers, and she smiled.

❖ ❖ ❖

Celia watched from the balcony, pleasantly stoned.

Moony looked confused.

The shrubs, an ornamental sort from China, were yellowing in parts. When he handled their waxy leaves to inspect for a possible infestation, they crumbled and fell off. He noticed several small clumps of browning leaves—he had assumed they were old blooms that had dropped after doing what they did, leaving seeds, possibly.

Using his hands to dig through the dirt at the base of the plant, he was surprised by an odd smell, like pesticide or tar. He used the maintenance radio Perry had given him—it had *Julio* markered onto its back—to ask whether anything had been sprayed on the bushes. Deb said no. He told her about the condition they were in but that she shouldn't worry; he would take care of them. He had seen an infestation like this before, ten-four, he said.

Only the west-facing bushes were showing any signs of sickness. He squinted west at the golf course. In the distance, a family of six wearing red shirts reading "Cartoon Animals" gave each other high-fives. He looked farther down the green. Two holes behind them, another group of six, wearing blue, shouted something like a warrior chant at the Cartoon Animals family.

It could be some sort of herbicide from the golf course, he thought. With these shrubs being foreign, they might be considered weeds by the herbicide, however that worked. He could ask the golf course maintenance people if they sprayed, but, he supposed, that wouldn't do any good now, unless there was some sort of antidote for shrubs. Instead, he counted the bushes. A total of seventeen might need replacing. He shook his head. That would mean a lot of digging—he hoped it wouldn't come to that.

He lit a cigarette. The springy sound of a large elastic band issued from the distance on the golf course. Moony looked up again and saw that the Cartoon Animals had been pelted with sky-blue toy arrows with suction cup heads. The blue family sat ducked behind a golf cart, shouting at the other family and cheering for themselves. Apparently they were done playing golf and had moved on to blood sports.

"You manure!" yelled the Cartoon Animals father in an impressive bass voice, clenching his hands into fists hard enough to crack his knuckles. His wife pulled off the arrow trembling from his perspiring brow. "Now you will be defeated."

The way the man said it—like he'd learned English from action movies—made Moony think of his wilderness survival instructor. Ex-military, probably. Maybe not. The guy had taught them to build debris huts and said things like "This is how you survive when the shit hits the fan." His father had called it tradecraft. But what the fuck is tradecraft, really? The other kids, he was pretty sure, just thought of it as camp.

Moony had spent that whole summer waiting for something that never happened. Some moment when the instructor would pull him aside and say, "Your father wanted me to show you the real stuff." But there was no real stuff. Just a bunch of rich kids learning to filter water through sand and charcoal.

Which to Moony meant that the training must have been so deep, so convincing, that even he couldn't tell where it ended and his own delusions began. Whoever had installed these reflexes, this way of seeing the world—he still wasn't remembering it all clearly. Maybe he'd never remember who'd actually trained him or when. But if living this deliberately small life—watering shrubs, mixing drinks, refusing every call to importance—was what all that preparation had been for, then it was working exactly as designed. The perfect undercover mission *would* look like nothing at all.

The Cartoon Animals dad motioned to his eldest son, who produced from a backpack a half dozen eyeball-design water balloons and handed them out to the rest of the Animals.

Moony sided with the Cartoon Animals. They were playing a game everyone could see. That was honest, at least.

The leader of the blue shirts, a lanky man in blue overalls and cap, barked at his army to reload. "Keep your eyes peeled; hit your mark."

There was no time for the blue-shirt assault. Some of them still wearing suction arrows, the Cartoon Animals inundated their cowering opponents. Every balloon hit its target in the face. The eyeball designs burst into a tasteless fog: a zombie-green hue of thick paint.

While the blue team recovered from the paint attack, the Cartoon Animals advanced, producing close-range weaponry constructed from hollow plastic.

"Rip off your shirt. Beat the shit out of those blue dorks," Moony muttered near the shrubs.

Sure enough, the Cartoon Animals patriarch unbuttoned his red shirt. It looked like a gesture of peace, maybe—he extended the shirt in his hand toward the blue father to wipe his face with.

The rest of the Cartoon Animals stood by, within striking distance. Beyond them, a stone's throw away, were three more blue-shirt kids. They unleashed a volley of grape-size firecrackers that crackled and spit yellow sparks. The stubby turf around the golf cart where both teams stood smoldered, and the paint let off an odd gas.

A girl in red was struck in the ear by a firecracker, and she ran, braids whipping her toward the little pond to cool her singed scalp. A little blue girl about the same age hopped out from behind the reeds and threw turquoise-painted eggs at her as the red girl dunked her head underwater. The eggs missed her head yet broke apart anyway on the surface of the water, pooling briefly before vanishing.

Moony felt something brush over his toe. He jerked his foot back and looked down to see he had flipped a small turtle on its back. As he leaned over to turn it upright, the turtle did so itself and headed in the opposite direction. It was white as a mountaintop.

The Cartoon Animals father stepped over the blue dad to rescue his daughter. The blue team took the opportunity to shoot their arrows at him. Several of them stuck to the seat of his shorts. They waited a moment, then tugged the fishing line attached to the suction cups and ripped open the back seam of his red shorts.

The Cartoon Animal kids dropped their weapons and ran to their sister and dad. At any rate, the game was over when the red grandfather, with a three-person slingshot from a nearby hill, pummeled the entire blue team with a massive balloon of paint that ruptured into a huge and oppressive pile. Assisting him was the blue-shirt father's wife and grandmother, who, both extremely attractive in their tight shirts, had become loyal to the Cartoon Animals.

❖ ❖ ❖

Beneath the base of one of the bushes sat the God pot.

Moony peered into it, seeing a cloudy reflection.

"Hey, *buddy*," a pale thirtysomething man screamed from across the C complex parking lot. The man, who looked like a figure on the Sistine Chapel ceiling, delicately watering miniature cacti, waved back, but the screaming man was gesturing with his pinkie-ringed right hand that Moony should hurry over.

A robin, coming out of the clear blue sky, swooped low in front of him on his way across the parking lot, so close that he could feel the wind displaced by its wings.

"Are you the *maintenance guy*?"

The pinkie ring had a large turquoise stone set into it.

"Nope," Moony answered, pawing at his gardening gloves.

"No?" the man asked again for verification.

Moony watched the man's knobby nose move. As the man looked Moony over, shaking his head with the importance of his situation, the nose wagged and bounced a little. It looked like it had been through a hailstorm or was made from primitive rubber.

Moony chose to answer that yes, he was the maintenance man.

"Well . . ." The man paused, "I was *needing* to get a *maintenance man* to look at my garbage disposal. It smells like a *trash can* in my apartment. Like *old food*. And it's because of the *drain* on the damned *garbage disposal*."

Moony took out his walkie-talkie, turning his face away from the tenant. "Deb," he said into it. He asked the man his apartment number. "There's a tenant here who has a complaint about his garbage disposal. He said his apartment smells."

Deb responded, "It's the weekend, sleepyhead. Tell him we'll fix it first thing Monday."

The man went red in the face.

Moony said, "Let me take a look at it, and I'll try and help."

✦ ✦ ✦

It really did smell like old food in the apartment of the man with the hail-damage nose. The standard Sod Hill faucet had been replaced with a brass Kohler model—it shone like gold. The rest of his place looked like the most boring apartment Moony had ever seen. Above the sink was a map of Colorado hung diagonally.

Moony, who didn't understand the slightest thing about plumbing, asked for a flashlight. He peered down the garbage disposal. Dirty things, both large and small, solid and liquid rested in the bottom of the cylinder. He turned it on, and it flung out pungent mucus into his mustache.

"The disposal works fine, no?" asked Moony.

"Yeah, it just *smells* bad."

Moony looked under the sink.

"That's your problem right there."

"*What* is?" the man asked.

"It's got a leak."

"Where?"

"Right there. See?"

"I'll be *damned*." The man's nose whistled as he exhaled relief. "*To boot*, I believe I'm the culprit. It must have taken *damage* from my trash can knocking against it. I shall patch that up myself. I'm glad it wasn't something *serious*. What's your name so I can recommend you to your supervisor?"

"Oh, that's not necessary."

"There aren't many good operators out there. I insist."

"Moony."

"Mookie," the man repeated.

"Sure, whatever."

"No, I mean it. People will respect a good one."

ABOUT THE AUTHOR

Stephen Lloyd Webber lives in Austin, Texas.

For updates on upcoming books and events, visit:
stephenlloydwebber.com and tmmw.io